VISIONS
IN LIGHT AND SHADOW

A Collection of
Science Fiction and Mystery Stories

By

John L. Flynn, Ph.D.

BrickHouse Books, Inc.
Baltimore, Maryland

BrickHouse Books, Inc.
541 Piccadilly Road
Baltimore, Maryland 21204

VISIONS IN LIGHT AND SHADOW:

A Collection of Science Fiction & Mystery Stories

By John L. Flynn, Ph.D.

PRINTING HISTORY
Second Edition / September 2019

Most of the stories have appeared, sometimes in slightly different form, in various magazines, which I am glad to acknowledge here:

Annapolis Review: "A Study in Evil" and "Solutions"
The Daily Planet: "Count on Doomsday"
Eldritch Tales: "Night of Passage"
Images: "The Second Apple"
Nexus: "The Jovian Dilemma," "A Gift of Verse"
and "Interfacing Rush"

Editor: Clarinda Harriss
Design & Layout: John L. Flynn

ISBN: 0-932616-68-2

PRINTED IN THE UNITED STATES OF AMERICA

10 9 8 7 6 5

Table of Contents

For Ray Bradbury, whose short fiction
inspired me to write,
and
For Martha Denny, whose patience as
a teacher helped me to refine
those skills.

Whom Gods Destroy

—■—

One of my favorite science fiction films is the 1956 M-G-M classic "Forbidden Planet," partially because it features one of the silver screen's great characters, Robby the Robot. Unlike the marauding, killer robots that appeared as his contemporaries, Robby was a gentle, loving mechanical man who served his flawed human masters. When he's instructed to harm a human in order to protect his master, Robby simply short-circuits; he is incapable of committing murder or other acts of mayhem. I had always wanted to give Robby a literary descendant, and when I began toying with the idea of creating a futuristic version of the Great Library at Alexandria, my robot librarian was born. Rupert owes much to Karel Capek's R.U.R. and Isaac Asimov's robots as well, but I like to think of him as Robby's step-son.

Rupert crawled out of the cave, scrambled onto a large metal pylon beside the entrance, and watched the sun paint the western sky. Night would soon be upon him, and he had to stay alert for the Old Ones. Sometimes he searched for them in the valley, and sometimes he searched for them in the cold, night sky, but always he listened. Listened for the soft, sweet, lyrical words and phrases which had given him a soul. In the morning, after yet another endless night of watching, and waiting, and listening, he returned to the cave.

For nearly three thousand years, Rupert had toiled without interruption and to all outward appearances without hesitation, serving and safeguarding the last great library on earth. Other than the handful of coworkers who long ago had ceased to function, he had known little else. The Library was his universe. Buried deep below the soft limestone rock of Missouri in an immense network of vaults, grottoes, and underground caverns, the Library contained the total accumulated knowledge of the human race from its primitive beginnings to the day of its annihilation. Gathered around him, painstakingly and meticulously preserved for future generations that would never be born, were the books, records, paintings, music, film, and history of a once great civilization. Rupert had not only catalogued every single item by hand as part of his service to the Library but had also committed each one to memory. When he had finished, he hungered for more of the Old Ones—their lyrical metaphors, their soft poetic melodies, their bold bright images—the triumph and tragedy that had been man. That hunger led him outside the thermostatically controlled, vacuum sealed, sterile world of the Library and had held him captive on the mountaintop for more than a million starlit vigils.

But this night's vigil was different, somehow. Once he had settled atop the pylon, Rupert barely stirred as the sun went down. Beyond the distant mountains in the east, the full moon was rising, and a cold, blustery wind was blowing down into the valley. Frost was already forming in some of the dark crevices and shadows. By nightfall, the frigid temperatures had turned the last droplets of moisture into thin patches of ice scattered across the plain, but the cold did not seem to matter to him. In the beginning, the cruel arctic winds had been a terrible reminder that he was nothing more than a confection of self-replicating neural networks, microprocessor-controlled relays, miniaturized components, wires, and a hyper-alloy body chassis. The finest in machine intelligence, not flesh and blood. But in time, as the long nights stretched into centuries, he had discovered other ways to feel the chill of the cold winds. Rupert imagined himself as Anna Karenina pulling her mink-lined cloak tight around her cold, rosy cheeks, or young Ishmael huddled next to the savage Queequeg in the cold lower depths of the Pequod, or the anonymous Ball Turret Gunner shivering, hunched in the belly of the B-17 bomber. He had learned what it meant to be cold from the books and records left behind by the Old Ones, even though he had never known the sensation himself. Tonight, for some unknown reason beyond his programming, he did not feel much like imagining.

Rupert looked out across the frozen valley to search for a sign of the Old Ones, but there was no trace at all. He then turned his   tired gaze to the heavens above, to the only tangible sign he had ever seen of them outside the great library. There, depicted in the enigmatic points of light, were the stories and fables the Old Ones had told about their gods. The hunter Orion with his faithful dog Sirius trailing behind him. Mighty Hercules, fair Andromeda, and fickle Cassiopeia. The Great Bear with its distant lights pointing to the Northern star. Once, with an immense effort that defied all the sub-routines of his neural-net processing, Rupert had traced their paths across the sky with his mechanical fingers, and tried to visualize each one of the celestial configurations in their imaginary forms. But on this particular night, he felt they mocked him with their cold indifference. In some vain, irrational effort to blot them out, he stretched out his hands high in the air, then suddenly stopped.

What he saw left him so paralyzed with disbelief that for long seconds he was unable to move. One of the tiny points of starlight had broken away from the constellation Orion and was moving northwesterly across the plane of the ecliptic. For years, he had tracked comets and shooting stars, or had witnessed stars erupt into life or wink out of existence, or had catalogued all manner of unidentified empyreal anomaly, but he had never seen anything like this. He studied the tiny point as it traversed the night sky, then watched as its faint starlight was engulfed by the blazing dawn.

Rupert sat there motionless, his shadow moving beneath him as the sun rose over the distant mountains, reached its zenith above the valley, and descended in the west. He had completely forgotten his duty to the Library. All that mattered to him was the tiny dot of light, and he remained alert, unmoving, with his eyes focused on its last known position in the sky until sunset. Then, as nightfall gave birth to a billion points of starlight, he found it again, a few centimeters or a hundred thousand miles to the left. Rupert did not jump for joy at his discovery. Nor did he feel relief or happiness, for such emotions were utterly beyond his understanding, but as he continued to follow the luminous flyspeck, he felt a dim sensation deep within his alloy frame. His circuits and relays seemed warmer than usual, and his neural pathways were flooded with repetitive commands and system errors.

Every night, for nearly a week, he watched the tiny point grow to brightness and dimension in the canopy of stars overhead. Then, more brilliant than any star, the dazzling point of light glided past the gas giants and swept by Mars. Finally, the star ship—for at last he had identified its distinctive shape and appearance as that of an interplanetary craft—settled into an orbit around the Earth. Once, then twice, it passed slowly across the sky, rising up to the zenith and descending into the west. *Any moment now*, the thought pulsed through Rupert's neural network with each subsequent pass, *they will fire their retro-rockets and start their landing*. He was so certain the automated radio beacon would guide their navigators to the Library, and him, that he scrutinized every orbit for the appropriate course correction. But that change in course never came. Instead the ship continued on its fixed path, traversing the heavens every ninety minutes until the dawn obliterated any trace of its existence.

Rupert watched and waited for another day and night. He did not know who they were or where they had come from, but his expectations were high. Ever since he had first crawled out of the Library and starred up at the night sky, he had so looked forward to meeting the Old Ones. To Rupert, they were like gods, for they had not only created him but also had filled him in a way that was utterly beyond his comprehension. Their music, their art, their poetry, and their fiction had held him captive for so many years that it was difficult for him to conceive of a world without them. Transfixed, he followed their passage in the heavens, his circuits and relays growing hotter with each revolution.

Then, at long last, the ship broke from its orbital path and started its descent. It flashed across the sky, glinting briefly from the borrowed rays of the sun, then landed with a roar in the valley below. The thin patches of ice turned instantly into pools of liquid then gaseous vapor. A few moments later the crew commander followed by two others emerged from the ship and moved slowly across the plain. They appeared to be dressed in heavy, environmental suits, not unlike the ones Rupert imagined Captain Nemo and his crew wore twenty-thousand leagues under the sea.

Rupert leaped from the pylon, and his metal feet hit the ground with a thud. He then scrambled down the almost vertical slope outside the cave, only slightly hindered by the loose rock and gravel that gave way under his weight. He looked again to see if his visitors were still in sight, but there was no trace of them in the valley. Perhaps he had frightened them off with his sudden appearance—Rupert recalled that's what had happened when Dr. Frankenstein's monster first appeared to the villagers of the small hamlet of Ingolstadt. But upon further inspection, he realized they had only temporarily vanished behind a large boulder. He continued down the incline, every one of his internal systems racing toward critical mass.

When he reached the bottom, they were already waiting. The three of them stood in a tight, defensive formation, the crew commander in front, flanked on either side by one of his men. Rupert had seen enough of the sports programs left behind by the Old Ones to wonder if they were readying for a meeting or a match. He slowed his pace, and switched his language program to the stand-by mode. Then, as the distance between them narrowed, he strained to look behind their opaque faceplates. They appeared humanoid—two arms, two legs, but he could tell little else. Was it too much to expect them to be the Old Ones?

"Greetings and salutations," he said with a bow and a flourish, borrowed largely from Dumas. "My designation is RU-242, but I am programmed to respond to the name Rupert." He waited for them to acknowledge his words, then added, "If you do not speak English, I am fluent in a hundred and eighty-seven other languages along with their various dialects and sub-tongues."

"Omigod," one of the two flanking crew members gasped, while the other exchanged a hurried glance, which did not go unnoticed by Rupert, and snapped to his commander's side with a weapon drawn. The commander fixed both of them with a cold stare, then took a step toward Rupert, filling his field of vision. "I am Captain Hrothgar," he said in a scratchy metal voice. "This is my first officer Farmon, and my science officer Ardith-Wyn Daedbot. We are licensed prospectors with the Coalition Trade Guild, and have been granted exclusive rights to the worlds in this system under the neutrality act of Proxima Three. Has a rival firm already contacted you—"

"Has anyone staked a claim here in this system?" Farmon interrupted, pushing Hrothgar aside.

"You speak English," Rupert observed, unaware that he had just been asked a direct question. When the question finally caught up to his neural processor, he replied with the only answer he knew: "I have been alone here for two thousand, nine hundred and eighty-six years."

"Alone all that time..." the captain sighed.

Farmon made a show of checking the sky and the distant mountains beyond, then holstered his weapon. "Where the hell are we? What piece of shit rock is this anyway?" he demanded answers from the science officer. "I thought you told us this system was uninhabited."

"That's what the scout ships reported," Daedbot snarled, checking the survey data against the information gathered from her hand-held scanner. "No sentient lifeforms on M-137C or any of the other rock in this system. We're at the hind-end of space, loverboy, with a big empty shovel stuck up our ass."

The first officer turned toward Daedbot, and pantomimed the action of drawing his weapon and firing point-blank at her. He then brought the weapon down to his faceplate and pretended to blow the smoke from its muzzle. Finally, he returned the imaginary weapon to his holster. Undaunted, she fired back with a singular gesture of her own. Then she raised her arms in the air and started dancing around in a circle like someone who had just scored the victory point in a hotly-contested match.

"M-137C," Hrothgar repeated, loud enough and clear enough to give pause.

"They called it, Earth," Rupert said, barely a whisper. He was still trying to compute and categorize their bizarre assortment of oscillations and locomotions when Farmon and Ardith-Wyn Daedbot suddenly stopped dead in their tracks. *Was it something I said?* he pondered, instantaneously reviewing the meager transcript of their encounter by examining each word and inflection.

The captain looked from faceplace to faceplate, and turned back to Rupert. He tried not to appear surprised, and kept the tone in his voice even, the words flat, with obvious effort. "I have been informed by my science officer that this planet's official designation is M-137C. Why do you refer to your world with a word that, in our language, means soil?"

"That was what they called it."

"They? The original inhabitants?" Hrothgar asked, the answer already beginning to dawn on him before he had even finished asking the question. "Then you're not one of them. What manner of being are you?"

"I am a construct . . . a fabrication," Rupert replied. "I was forged from the finest metals and alloys, built on an assembly line in Detroit, fashioned in the likeness of the men and women who created me, and brought to life on September 6, 2054, at a research facility in San Jose. I spent my electronic childhood at the University of Chicago, and went to work as an information specialist for the Ark Project shortly thereafter."

Farmon shouted, "A goddamn robot!"

"I prefer the term 'synthetic being,'" Rupert hastened to add. "The word 'robot' has such negative connotations. Originally, it derived from a Czechoslovakian term used to refer to slave labor—"

"Shut up, or I'll switch you off."

"That's enough, Farmon—"

"I don't think so, sir," he snorted. "According to the provisions of the Briggs-Meyer Settlement, robots have no legal status as sentient beings. They are not entitled to own property or negotiate contracts. That means we are under no legal obligation to negotiate a claim or share a goddamned thing with him."

"I'm fully acquainted with the regulations," Hrothgar returned.

"Well, maybe you need to look at them again," Farmon said, thumping his captain's breastplate with the tips of his gloved fingers. He paused long enough to consider his actions, then turned to walk away. "Besides I am tired of listening to this bucket of bolts. There ain't no such place as Earth. That's just some goddamned fairy-tale for children——"

Hrothgar's voice overlapped his first officer's. "Rupert, is there anyone else still left alive on this planet?"

"No, I am all that remains of the human race."

"Doesn't look like much of a going concern," Farmon interjected.

The captain ignored him, and pressed Rupert for some more answers. "What happened? A war?"

"No, there was no war."

"A plague?"

"No, there was no plague."

"An invasion?" he continued his interrogation.

"A natural disaster," Ardith-Wyn Daedbot stated, reporting her sensor readings.

"An act of God," Rupert corrected her, completely unaware how illogical his statement must have sounded to the seasoned space travelers. "Scientists had long speculated about the disaster which had caused the extinction of the great reptiles that once held dominion over the Earth. But when astronomers on two continents concluded that a comet—a comet so massive that its impact would cause mass extinction and long-term, global climate changes—was on a collision course with the Earth, the debate was over. Mankind was about to go the way of the dinosaur, and nothing in his great arsenal of science and technology could save him.

"Attempts were made to preserve the species by sending thousands of volunteers—all rugged individualists—in huge colony ships to the nearest star. The billions of others who remained behind were crowded into underground bunkers and shelters of every imaginable shape and size. Efforts were also undertaken to safeguard all manner of livestock, vegetation, political leadership, technology, and culture. But in the end, it wasn't enough. The comet struck the far side of the planet on December 25, 2061. Billions of tons of dust and water vapor were hurled into the atmosphere, forming a cloud that surrounded the earth and blocked out all sunlight for years. Robbed of solar radiation, most plant and sea life died; the animals that fed on the plants then starved to death. Those humans who had survived the initial blast and the acid rains and freezing temperatures that followed soon consumed the last of their supplies, and began to feed on each other until there was no one left. By the time the great dust shroud settled, Earth was very much a dead world.

"This planet," he concluded, "was once the cradle of a great and illustrious civilization. Now all trace of man and his works has vanished from the surface. Even his great cities, with their cloud-piercing towers of glass and steel, have crumbled back into the soil. All that remains, buried deep within these rocks, is the last of his great and magnificent labors—the Library."

"A library? You must be joking," Farmon exclaimed.

"More than just a library," he said, an inflection of pride slipping into his automated, highly-logical response program. "A vast storehouse of learning and culture like no other in recorded history."

Captain Hrothgar fixed his gaze upon the robot, but made no sound or movement.

"Come," Rupert insisted, "I will show you all that is left of the moments, men, and places."

Rupert led his visitors down into the cave and through the first entrance to the subterranean cavern. The vault door slid shut behind them, and the vacuum seals sucked out the gas in its titanium frame with a loud hiss. He then keyed several commands into a control panel, and the men in their pressure suits were jolted and jarred by a thunderous blast of air. Without apparent thought or deliberation, Farmon grabbed for his weapon, but the captain restrained him from drawing it out of the holster; the science officer simply quivered in silence, her arms wrapped tightly around the handle to the vault door. Rupert observed their odd mixture of behaviors, and struggled to reconcile them with what he had known of Shakespeare, or Ghandi, or Beethoven, or DeMille, or any of the Others.

Once the airlock had completed its pressurization cycle, Rupert indicated that it was safe for them to take off their helmets and discard their environmental suits. They hesitated for a moment, while the science officer verified the robot's assessment, then they started peeling away the heavy, cumbersome layers—captain first, followed by the other two. When his visitors finally did remove their helmets, he glimpsed their faces for the first time. They looked human, but not like any human he had ever seen before. Their features were gaunt, cadaverous, shadows filling the deep crevices in place of flesh and muscle. Their eyes like those of the deep-water predators were cold and lifeless, and their hair resembled dried straw that had been trampled on a field. *We are the stuffed men/Leaning together/Headpiece filled with straw/Shade without color*, Rupert recalled T.S. Eliot. These were the hollow men, and nothing like the Old Ones.

Rupert opened and latched back the inner vault door, pointing out its high molecular density and explaining how it could be sealed against all attempts to enter. He then led them down a long, narrow corridor toward the nerve center of the library, their footsteps echoing in the solemn stillness. Eventually, they reached an archway which opened onto a much larger chamber, and he saw in their faces the dawning of incomprehensible awe and incredulous wonder. Stooping, he led them through, then stood aside to watch them as they had their first sight of the great library. They gazed, and gaped, and glared, disbelieving, struck silent like children faced by a first glimpse of Christmas morning.

"This is the Library's nerve center," Rupert reported, as a matter of fact. "By no means the largest of the nearly four-thousand, six-hundred and fifty vaults, galleries, and subterranean compartments, but infinitely the most important. From here, you can access the total accumulated knowledge of the human race from its primitive beginnings to the day of its annihilation."

"Four-thousand, six-hundred and fifty other chambers just like this one," the science officer said, the look of incredulity reshaping her emaciated features like clay in the hands of a sculptor. "And you've managed this entirely on your own?"

"No, there were twelve of us originally," he replied, the tone of his words softer and filled with great reverence. Rupert let them stare for a while before he spoke, and when he did continue, he was careful to keep his narrative simple and factual. "Each of us were programmed to serve a different part of the

Library. My area was poetry and fiction. Over the course of time, three developed mechanical problems, two perished in a fire which destroyed part of the media wing. Several others contracted computer viruses, and three just stopped. After the fire, the Library decided we should convert most of the materials to computer files. Those of us who remained worked on this arduous task for decades, and when it was finally complete, I was the last one still functioning."

"Unbelievable," she sighed.

"It's incredible," Captain Hrothgar exclaimed, turning around in a circle, struggling to take in every last unimaginable detail.

The Library's central chamber was immense. Stretching back into the shadowy distance, as far and farther than their eyes could reach, an almost infinite repetition of bookcases—side by side, head to foot—housed a million or more books in their gleaming metal shelves. In the center, illuminated by an unseen source of light, a reflecting pool and marble fountain stood. Pillars and columns, which had been carved and sculpted by artisans several thousand years before, were spaced at even intervals around its perimeter. At the far end, directly across the chamber from the tunnel entrance where they stood, the columns supported a massive balcony whose richy-ornamented frieze work depicted the march of human history. Beneath each cornice, the frieze work continued in provocative shapes, distorted by the play of light and shadow. Many statues and busts of forgotten heroes and politicians and gods adorned finely-decorated alabaster pedestals. In a small alcove just beyond thecentral chamber, the walls were covered with masterpieces by Rembrandt, Picasso, and Matisse. Another alcove contained a consultation desk, with a huge, shimmering, transparent computer display.

Rupert led them to the consultation desk, and keyed a seriesof commands into the computer. "Here," he explained pointing at a holographic projection of the architectural blueprints of the Library. "Here, in these various caves and caverns, lies the protected history of mankind, the cherished words and pictures of all that humans once knew and loved . . ."

The captain and his crew crowded closer, and Rupert paused

long enough for them to get a clear look at the image on the computer display. Their eyes were only watchful. He could see no light of comprehension or even simple understanding in them. They were like children watching a magician perform his easy bag of tricks and not grasping how effortless the slight of hand was for him. Rupert knew deep within his alloy frame he must somehow make them understand.

". . . the safe and dear upholstered memories," he continued, identifying the various sections of poetry and biography and literature. Then, with a sudden burst of inspiration, he shrugged aside the computer display and pantomimed one of his favorite stories from Shakespeare. "Consider the noble Moor who threw a pearl of beauty away richer than all his tribe . . . Ahab and his mad search for the great white whale . . . Tom and Huck . . . Gatsby in white flannels holding Daisy . . . Arthur and Guinevere and Lancelot . . . sweet, orphaned Cosette . . ." One by one, Rupert related their stories, by harpooning imaginary beasts, or white-washing illusory fences, or dancing fanciful steps, or slaying fantastical dragons, or rescuing apparitional children. He labored more than hour and a half, entertaining them like some grand magician, with only a handful of gestures.

Finally, Captain Hrothgar interrupted him. "You claim this . . . this library has been here for some three thousand years," he said, turning the attention back to the holographic display, "but this equipment—this technology—everything—it seems so new! As if it had been here only a few years instead of centuries—"

"Everything you see here, Captain," Rupert replied, weary, lacking the sparkle and vitality that had possessed him moments before, "has stood unchanged since its original conception three millennia ago."

"I'd say we hit the jackpot," Farmon interjected.

"What are you talking about?"

"Com'on, Captain. Take a look around," he said, taking his superior's arm and pulling him aside. "These books are worthless, but will you look at all that equipment? It is ancient, and hardly state-of-the-art, but you know, on some third world, backwater planet, this stuff would fetch a pretty prize."

"Yeah, we could be rich," the science officer added.

Hrothgar looked shocked. "This is an important archeological discovery that needs to be brought to the attention of the Coalition."

Farmon shook his head. "Captain, may I remind you that we're prospectors, not archeologists. Prospectors," he said, repeating the word with greater emphasis. "In my book, that's just a fancy way of saying scavengers. We make our living picking the bones of dead things clean, and I haven't seen anything deader than this library in a half a dozen worlds."

Rupert watched and listened from afar, like the shy girl in the school window who hadn't been invited to her high school dance. He noted their every move and gesture, and heard every word they said, but the complexities and contradictions of human interaction were beyond his basic programming. He had only a dim awareness.

"Farmon's right, Captain," she said. "We signed onto this expedition to make money, not discoveries. Leave that to the eggheads back home."

"The existence of Rupert, and this library, proves the theories about the existence of a mother-world from which all the great corporate dynasties descended," Hrothgar said, his eyes bright with excitement. "We've always thought Earth was a myth—some fairy-tale parents told their children at night—but our discovery proves that it really did exist. Just think, we could change the whole make-up of the Coalition. With this one discovery, we could set everything back."

"Great," Farmon replied, raising his arms in the air and shaking his hands, "the find of a lifetime, and all it's worth is a fuckin' pat on the back. Yeah, we'll get our pictures on all the vids, do the talk-show circuit, but when we finally do get back here—"

"—the place is crawling with all manner of scientists and archeologists, not to mention the religious fanatics who are looking for some sign of God," Daedbot completed his sentiment.

The first officer grinned at her. "No thanks!" he said to the captain.

"You can count me out," she added.

Hrothgar frowned, all at once keenly aware of the robot's presence. "We'll finish this discussion back at the ship," he said, checking time on his chronometer. "We've got a tight schedule to keep, and we're not going to waste valuable time arguing about it now. We'll have nine months on the return trip to settle things, one way or the other. Is that agreed?"

Farmon and Daedbot nodded their agreement.

"Rupert, was there more to this library you wanted to show us?" the captain asked.

"Yes . . . yes!" he replied, animated like Pinocchio without strings. "Please follow me."

*   *   *   *   *

The next day, Rupert crawled out of his cave at the first sight of dawn and waited for them at the base of the mountain. He waited and watched and listened for several hours as the day wore on. The sun, bright and hot, burned away the last pools of ice, and threw shimmers of light in the distance. At first, Rupert imagined he could see them running from far off beyond the plain, but then he thought it was only a mirage, a heat-induced atmospheric refraction of light. He turned away, shook off the image, and looked again. But there it was again, only closer. The captain was out in front. Behind him were two space-suited figures trying to keep pace. When Hrothgar finally reached Rupert, he was out of breath.

"Good day, Captain Hrothgar."

"Hello, Rupert," he replied, panting, still trying to catch his breath. "I have to talk to you—"

Just then, both Farmon and Daedbot came racing up, and collapsed to their knees in exhaustion. The first officer gulped down the air in his helmet, and exhaled his words, "Would you mind telling us what that was all about? What's with all the rush?"

"Not that it's any business of yours, Farmon," he replied, still breathing hard, "but I wanted a moment alone with the robot."

"Don't sugarcoat it, Captain. Just tell him straight."

Hrothgar turned away from his first officer, and looked at

Rupert. "We've come to take you with us," the captain said, his voice flat and lifeless.

Rupert studied the anonymous faceplates of the crew, and took a step back from them.

"I didn't want to tell you this way, but now you know. Let's not make it any tougher on the two of us than it has to be," he added. The captain had straightened himself up, and was now breathing normally. "We have to take off from here in less than fifteen hours. We can't wait any longer than that, or we'll miss our launch window, and we simply don't have enough supplies to last us until the next available launch time."

"But my work here at the Library—" Rupert pleaded, pointing to the top of the mountain.

"We don't have time for this," the science officer reminded them.

Captain Hrothgar grunted. "Look, Rupert. We can't risk leaving you behind. If we found you, then others might find you as well—"

"Others?" he repeated.

"Yes, others, and they won't be licensed prospectors like us. They'll be claim-jumpers or scavengers, or worse, and they'll stop at nothing, including ripping your library apart and selling its pieces off to the highest bidders, just to get what they want."

Rupert felt a strange, icy chill moving through his alloy frame.

"Now, we don't have a whole lot of time," Hrothgar said in a low voice as he advanced toward the robot. "You must pull your personal belongings together, and get ready to move out by dawn." He paused, and lowered his head. "One more thing . . . my ship is a survey ship, not a passenger liner. We weren't expecting to pick anybody up, just maybe a few rock samples. We've only got room for about twenty pounds of stuff, so you better pick up what you need most and leave the rest of it behind."

Rupert stopped moving. In the redundant sub-processors of his neural network, realization had come to him. His lips formed the words "Twenty pounds" Then he whispered them aloud, "Twenty pounds." And finally, he said, "Twenty pounds! I've got more than twenty pounds of books. How can I possibly choose between them? Would you force a mother to choose between her children?"

"Books!" Farmon exclaimed. "We don't have room for your books. We only got room enough for you, your repair kit, your battery charger, or whatever it is you use for power, and maybe a tooth brush."

"I can't leave them behind," Rupert pleaded. "I can't abandon my duty to the Library.

"You're not exactly being given a choice here, tin man."

"Farmon, that's enough. I'll handle this."

"Whatever you say, sir," the first officer replied, drawing his weapon out of its holster and adjusting its sights on the robot.

He shook his head slowly back and forth. "I am sorry, Rupert. I don't have any choice," the captain said. "Don't you understand. They haven't given me a choice. Your continued presence here on this world represents a very real threat."

"I have been alone here for two thousand, nine hundred and eighty-six years, and in all that time, your ship was the only one I ever saw."

"There will be others."

"Yes . . . the Old Ones."

Hrothgar shook his head again. "We are the Old Ones, Rupert. With all the petty jealousies, insecurities, and weaknesses that make us human. We are the descendants of that handful of rugged individualists who took to the stars so long ago—"

Rupert stared at him, aghast. His voice shook. "No, you're nothing like them."

"Yes, we are! Take a good, close look," the captain demanded, filling the robot's field of vision. "We are the flawed, imperfect beings who built that great, magnificent library. That was meant to be our legacy, our one great and noble gift to the universe. So that, if mankind did perish, others might one day know about the indomitable human spirit that strived for such great heights, for those books in there were written by men, not gods. Their words, their ideals that you hold so dear, are what we as humans aspire to, but not who we are—"

Rupert backed away, his hyper-alloy body chassis feeling suddenly cold. He turned and ran toward the cave, scrambling up the vertical slope. Hrothgar was right behind him, with Farmon and Daedbot in close pursuit. He clambered on all fours, but his metal feet kept sliding out from under him on the loose rock and gravel. He struggled to gain a foothold, little by little inching his way to the top of the mountain. Then, just as he was about the reach the summit, a loose boulder gave way, and Rupert lost his footing altogether. He toppled sideways on the slope and went plummeting down the far side.

Hrothgar climbed back down, then walked slowly and deliberately, over to him. Like Farmon, he had carried a weapon on his belt. He unfastened the safety clasp of the holster as he walked. "Rupert," he said, "you've got to understand this." He stopped a few feet from him. His voice crackled through the faceplate. "I don't have any choice. You've got to come back with us."

He took his weapon out of the holster, and held it up.

Rupert turned to him, still on his knees. "I can't abandon my post," he pleaded, crawling toward the captain. "I was programmed to care for the Library. I have a responsibility—"

His pleas were drown out by Farmon's arrival. "I told you he would run," he said, still panting.

"Captain, if the robot refuses to come with us, then you have to destroy him," the first officer reminded him. "There are no other options."

Hrothgar, looking down at the weapon in his hand, nodded. "Come on, Rupert," he said softly. "You have no choice but to come with us."

Rupert let the captain take his elbow, and help him to his feet. The four of them walked across the plain toward the space ship. About half way to the ship, Rupert paused, turning slowly to stare back at the metal pylon and hidden entrance to the Library. He could not cry except those silent tears that came from deep within. Hrothgar turned him back around and lead him to the ship that awaited them in the distance.

That night, the captain locked Rupert in the cargo hold of the ship, while he and his crew completed their final preparations for launch. But in the morning, less than an hour before take-off, he opened the cargo hold and saw that the robot was gone.

Captain Hrothgar came looking for him, with his weapon drawn. When he reached the top of the summit, he found Rupert standing in the entrance of the cave. "Now we can do this the hard way or the easy way," he said, his voice was flat and dull.

"I don't suppose you could go back to the ship, and tell the others you didn't find me."

"You know I can't do that."

"Just thought I'd ask," the robot said.

"Please, Rupert, don't make this any harder than—" the captain started to say, but never was able to complete his sentence.

For at that moment a huge, earth-shattering explosion, accompanied by a half dozen minor concussions, filled the valley with a cacophony of echoes. Instantly, the plain and the distant mountains beyond were scorched black as a cinder by a flash brighter than a hundred suns. Rupert and Captain Hrothgar both watched in awe as the wreckage and debris from the ship bloomed into a mighty mushroom cloud greater than the tallest mountains. Then they felt the shock waves crash down upon them. Everything happened in the space of a few short moments.

"What the hell was that?" Hrothgar asked, but he was already aware of the answer.

"I just destroyed your space ship," Rupert said, as a matter of fact.

The captain came up and sat down on a warm boulder, not looking at Rupert. "Why did you blow up my ship?"

"Several thousand years ago, before the great cataclysm destroyed the planet," Rupert explained, "peasant workers who felt their livelihood threatened by the introduction of automation tossed their wooden shoes, which were called 'sabos,' into the machines to stop them. Hence the word 'sabotage.'" He paused for some sign of acknowledgment, then concluded, "When I realized you had neglected to secure the cargo door properly, I was able to free myself. After that, it wasn't very difficult for me to sabotage your ship's reactor and steal away into the night while you were so busy getting ready for your launch."

"I think I understand," he replied. For a moment, the captain sat there in reflective silence, then he climbed to his feet. The hot sun beat down on his faceplate, a warm wind blowing up from the valley.

"Where's that goddamned traitorous robot!" Farmon yelled as he ran uphill and vaulted over the summit with his weapon drawn.

Without apparent thought, Hrothgar aimed his weapon at the first officer. Then he put it down, and stared at it for another long, silent moment. "I gave you strict orders to stay with the ship," he said, the weapon limp in his right hand.

"Yeah, well, if we ever get back home, you can bring me up on charges for disobeying your orders."

"Count on it!"

Farmon hesitated, then continued walking towards the two of them. "I knew you didn't have the stomach to kill him," he said, "so I'm here to finish the job."

"Lower your weapon," the captain ordered. "Killing the robot now is pointless."

"Pointless for you maybe, but I've got a score to settle with him."

"Get out of here, Rupert," Hrothgar shouted, placing himself in the line of fire between Farmon and the robot. "Go back down into your library, and read your fine books. I'll take care of this."

Rupert did not move from his position.

"Go on, now, before it's too late."

"What do you think you're doing?" the first officer demanded. "You can't let him get away. If he goes back down there, we'll never get him out."

"That's right." At last, Hrothgar had found the strength in his hand to raise his weapon. "He belongs down there in that sheltered world of high-minded ideals and noble principles. He is that immortal part that separates us from our bestial past, and he certainly doesn't deserve to die."

"And what happens to us?"

"Without supplies, a shelter, and air to breathe, we'll be dead in a couple of days, more or less."

"Get out of my way."

"No, you'll have to go through me to get to him."

"But why? Why is he so important that you'd be willing to risk your life to protect him?" Farmon pleaded with his captain for an answer.

"I'm not entirely sure," he said, distant, "but I seem to remember an old children's story my mother used to tell me about a pirate king and his buried treasure. After he had looted a rival's ship, this pirate would often dispatch a few of his men to bury his treasure in a predetermined spot, then would murder each of them in order to preserve his secret. Later, when he was asked why he did it, he claimed that 'dead men tell no tales.'"

"*Treasure Island* by Robert Louis Stevenson," Rupert interjected.

Hrothgar turned to nod at him, and suddenly, instantly, Farmon came charging up, screaming in fury. "Then die, you sonuvabitch!"

The captain drew a deep breath, and pulled the trigger. The blast from his weapon echoed in the valley and against the distant mountains, sending the loose rock and gravel scurrying for cover. Hrothgar never heard the sound, nor did Farmon hear his shot. Both had fired at the same time, and both had felt, for only an instant, the fatal fury of the other's deadly weapon.

Rupert squatted down by the captain's silent body, and cradled him in his metallic arms. He watched as the soil turned blood red under Hrothgar. "Perhaps, a thousand years from now," he spoke to the dead man, "when the human race has finally crawled back up to where they once stood in their great moment of triumph and tragedy, the Library with all its wondrous treasures will be waiting to be rediscovered. And on that great and glorious day, my friend, you will be remembered as one of the Old Ones who fought to preserve and protect it."

He buried their bodies in unmarked graves, and disposed of what remained of their ship's wreckage. When he had completed his grim task, Rupert strapped on Captain Hrothgar's weapon and climbed atop the metal pylon outside the entrance to the cave.

There, from the last light of day to the dim light of dawn, he watched, and waited, and listened for some sign of the Others. In the morning, after a long, cold night's vigil, he returned to his duties in the Library.

For Rupert, a thousand years did not seem like a long time to wait.

A Study in Evil

Are human beings, as certain religious groups would have us believe, innately evil, or are we sometimes possessed by evil forces when we commit horrible acts or atrocities? The late comedian Flip Wilson often said in jest, "The devil made me do it," but perhaps his words were more than simply a punchline. Clearly, something sets the Adolph Hitlers or the Ted Bundys of the world apart from the rest of humanity. If it is possible for heavenly angels to play a decisive role in the lives of certain human beings, then why not devils as well? "A Study in Evil" is a short, short story, more a rumination on the question of evil than the final answer.

The old man had died in the ghetto.

Too proud to receive the parish or community help, he had eaten every article of clothing he possessed, scraped off and devoured every scrap of plaster on the walls of his wretched room, gnawed his finger nails to the bone, and died, raging at God.

But though the old man was dead, the demonic presence inside him lived on.

* * * * *

Years before, as an impetuous youth, the demonic presence had annoyed his father with continual requests to study the evil side of human behavior. He argued that, if he were to take over the Firm someday, he wanted to learn about lust and pride and all those other mortal sins first hand. He longed to feel the pains of humanity that had made his father so infamous and to sign a few hapless individuals to the contract that had made the Firm so financially successful.

Finally, after centuries of listening to his son beg, plead and generally make his life miserable, his father reluctantly agreed. He had only one stipulation; he warned his son not to have any direct contact with Christian icons, as that would result in such an apocalyptic cataclysm that he would be destroyed.

The demonic presence agreed to his father's terms and departed, instantly forgetting what he had promised. Within a few decades, he had learned more about evil that most demons his age. He learned about hatred and violence from a small, brush war he started in Southeast Asia; lying, cheating and eracing tapes from a break-in he had arranged at a large, Washington hotel; avarice and greed from a powerful, oil cartel in the Middle East; lust from a Hollywood madam and her famous clients; deceit from a U.S. President and his mistress, and loneliness and despair from an old man in the New York ghetto.

*   *   *   *   *

The demonic presence climbed out and examined the old man's body with caution. He felt satisfied, having experienced the dying man's desperation. And yet, he sensed that there was still something missing from his study of the New York ghetto.

Suddenly, he heard the sound of breaking glass and tucked himself back in the old man's body, hungering for more of humanity's pain and suffering.

The demonic presence watched as an agile, young male of African-American extraction crawled through the broken window and ransacked the small room. He had often heard the old man complaining about black welfare recipients and the roving bands of street punks that had made living in uptown Manhattan so dangerous. He even remembered hearing him complain about a neighborhood youth who had recently broken into a local parish, and robbed the priest of his holy sacraments. He considered the young, black male, observing his quick, cat-like moves and his anti-social behavior. Perhaps he could learn more about oppression, racial bigotry and theft from this new subject.

Thinking fast, the demonic presence planted a slight suggestion in the youth's mind, then clung tightly to the old man's pocket watch. And when the black male took it, he followed the watch into the thief's black bag.

*   *   *   *   *

The black bag was not particularly big, and was not really

unique in any outward, physical appearance. Glimpsed by any street person, it would have looked like a simple black bag. The contents of the bag were really what gave it importance, for it contained the dozens of religious artifacts recently stolen from a neighborhood parish.

As the black youth climbed back to the fire escape, he smiled with great satisfaction. His score had been another profitable one. Little did he know that his simple act of larceny would have such an ironic and cataclysmic conclusion.

In the night sky, far above his head, the stars were already swirling in a tornadic frenzy.

The Jovian Dilemma

The late Carl Sagan suggested in his book Cosmos *that alien life was likely to be so different from what had evolved on earth that we might not recognize it as sentient, or even a true life form. And yet, most contemporary science fiction still envision alien life as largely humanoid in appearance and clearly capable of speaking our very complex language. Think about it—the aliens in "Star Trek" and most other stories all look the same, except for make-up appliances on their noses or foreheads, and speak colloquial English! What an egocentric view of the universe we humans possess! With that in mind, I set out to create a life form that was totally alien in its form and its thought-processes, and the result, "The Jovian Dilemma," was a first contact story between humans and this very different form of life.*

The colossal weather systems and the rotating bands of clouds, forever weaving a snakeskin tapestry of white, red and brown, had long since hidden the fact that Jupiter was inhabited.

For nearly a billion years, the inhabitants had thrived in the turbulent currents and eddies of an atmosphere rich in hydrogen, helium, methane, water and ammonia. But they themselves had no perception of the gas giant that was their home or, for that matter, the passage of the long centuries that defined their lifespan. They also had no real sense of racial or cultural identity, no notion of the fierce evolutionary struggle that had been waged over the millennium for their survival, and no awareness that, as a species, they were already far down the road to extinction. They simply existed, lazily floating in an updraft over one of the planet's many storm systems or propelling themselves through a mighty maelstrom to eat the precious few organic molecules that remained.

They probably evolved from one of those organic molecules, a single-celled life-form spewed up from some volcanic eruption deep within the planet and flushed into some sluggish backwater.

Since there was no accessible solid surface, but rather a dense, cloudy atmosphere, they tried to adapt to life at this lower level. But extremes in temperature and atmospheric pressure forced some of the more ambitious to seek refuge elsewhere. The first of them only lived long enough to carry offspring to the higher and cooler layers of the atmosphere before sinking back into the lower depths under their own tremendous weight. But others who were lighter and faster eventually followed. Those that reached the higher elevations and learned how to float survived; those that remained behind simply perished in the heat or the pressure of the gas giant.

The floaters soon learned to propel themselves through the atmosphere by expanding and then contracting planetary gases. With no formal knowledge of physics or chemistry, they could not even begin to comprehend what they were doing, but nonetheless they refined their technique to an artform. Gradually, as the countless eons passed, the lack of natural predators not only allowed their numbers to flourish but also made them very complacent. Satisfied with their limited accomplishments, they ignored the threat of famine their increasing numbers wrought. They were not concerned with hunger because they had never known it, and permitted complacency to make them very, very lazy. Little did they realize, their lack of concern had doomed them all to extinction. But most were content to float in great idle herds, processing food until they were too heavy to remain aloft, while so very few others continued to dance carelessly from cloud to cloud.

When the first faint glow of an interplanetary probe entered the Jovian system, Cloud-Dancer turned his attention towards the heavens. He did not know that this strange visitor had come from a distant neighbor, for such a conclusion was utterly beyond his understanding; but as he followed the ever-changing light in the sky he felt a dim disquiet that he and others like him had never before experienced. They knew nothing about apprehension and fear, love and hate, murder and greed. And yet, by the time he reached middle age, Cloud-Dancer knew more about his distant neighbors than he cared to know.

Mitchell Ryan stared, mesmerized, out the small porthole of the *Montgolfier* as the Great Red Spot of Jupiter began to swallow his fragile craft whole. The great column of gas reached high above the adjacent clouds, and reduced his bathyscaphe to a tiny, insignificant speck in an area large enough to contain half a dozen Earths. At over a million years old, the gigantic storm system afforded him a rare glimpse into the inferno that must have once given birth to moons, planets, stars and whole galaxies. Somewhere behind him, he knew, an orbiting space station and the faint flicker of light that was home were receding into the vast obscurity of space.

"No other view like it in the entire solar system," the pilot remarked.

Ryan turned from the porthole and grunted. His face was as pale as a white linen shroud.

"You know, we're not actually going down into the Eye," the pilot added. She flicked several switches to bring the craft around and then stretched to look out the porthole herself. "We're descending to that blue area just to the right, but we use the air currents and updrafts from the Eye to slow our descent." She slid back into her seat, and fingered several buttons that caused the craft to shudder like an elevator that had slipped between floors. "You wouldn't think so—what with that raging motherfucker of a storm below us. But there's actually much less turbulence than if we had descended over one of the bands, and this way we also avoid the clouds that are composed mainly of ammonia crystals."

"What the hell's going on?" Ryan demanded, as a sinking feeling in his stomach made him recall the first time he took a smoke.

"Just routine. Nothing to worry about."

"Why are we suddenly slowing?"

"We have to cycle over to another mixture while the cabin adjusts to the ambient pressure," she responded. The pilot adjusted several controls above her head, and Ryan felt a hiss sound pierce his inner eardrums. "We used to pressurize the ship entirely with helium, but people kept complaining about how cold it got and how it made their voices sound like Mickey Mouse. So now, we use a rather exotic mixture of gases."

Sliding out of his seat, Mitchell Ryan squeezed next to the pilot for a better look at the instruments. They were covered with moisture, and she had to keep rubbing the condensation away from the video display terminals with a cloth rag in order to read them.

Ryan rubbed his arms up and down with the palms of his hands as the small, four-man cabin became noticeably cooler to him. "And how does this pressurization affect the air we breathe?" he asked.

"We don't breathe air down here."

"Why not?"

"For the same reason you don't breath it on the thirteen-month trip from Earth," she answered, with a sigh. "Pure oxygen under pressure is pretty toxic, and at the depths we're descending, breathing the twenty-one or so percent oxygen you're used to on the Station is like taking a shower with hydrochloric acid. You'd burn the insides of your lungs right out—"

"So, what are we supposed to breathe then?"

"Down here, you breathe about two percent oxygen and ninety-eight percent other gases," she replied.

Mitchell Ryan stared off into space.

After a moment of thought, he spoke again. "I suppose that's what the miners, engineers and other members of my team will be breathing when they're aboard the mining platform?" he asked.

"You can't exist down here without it."

Ryan gulped down a deep breath. "Any risks to long term exposure?"

The pilot grinned at him over her shoulder. "Take your pick," she said, tugging the glove off her right hand and counting down with her fingers. "You've got nitrogen narcosis; if your mixture is the slightest bit off, you either get a good high, or you just fall asleep and never wake up. You've got decompression sickness, more commonly known as the bends. Then you've got oxygen toxemia, in which too much oxygen in the bloodstream poisons all of your healthy cells—"

Mitchell Ryan had to admit to himself that he had not fully considered any, or all, of these factors when he agreed to take over the project. He had allowed himself to be seduced by notions of power and prestige, and had failed to consider the human factor. Issues related to occupational safety, health and workman's compensation had completely eluded him.

"—and finally," she concluded, "the grand daddy of them all, High Pressure Nervous Syndrome, in which you simply go wacko."

"Wacko?" he stuttered, shaking his head.

"Yeah, tremors, nervousness, disorientation, paranoia-the whole men-in-white-labcoats thing. Wacko." The pilot punched another set of buttons, then continued, "HPNS affects nearly one in twenty people; although its debilitating symptoms rarely prove fatal, most victims never fully recover from long term exposure. Their minds just sort of turn into jello. That's why we make it a point to work no more than six hours on, and then a full forty-two hours off. You got a problem with that, you'll have to take it up with the union."

Without warning, the *Montgolfier* rolled to one side, and then plummeted down, like a falling elevator out of control.

"No—" he replied, stumbling back into his passenger seat, the words shaking out of his mouth, "—I hadn't even thought about it."

"We've completed our initial pressurization, and are now headed down," she reported, with a snicker. "We still have to make a couple of adjustments before we reach the Platform, but I figure we'll be there in less than twenty minutes or so." The pilot looked up at one of the computer monitors above her head, and flicked several switches on her command console. She then glanced over her shoulder. "Just try to sit back, and enjoy the ride."

*   *   *   *   *

Mitchell Ryan's face had turned from pale to ashen by the time they reached the mining platform deep within the atmosphere of Jupiter. The queasy sensation he had felt earlier in his stomach had climbed into his throat, and was threatening to explode all over the pressurized cabin of the *Montgolfier*. But he somehow managed to contain it by the sheer force of his will. He simply waited, with his eyes closed, for the ordeal to be over.

The sound of metal clanging against metal and the sharp jolt of mass reacting against mass meant that the craft was at last safely docked on the platform. Ryan breathed out a deep sigh of relief, and relaxed back in his seat. He sat there quietly, thoughtfully, while the pilot scrambled to open the hatch.

A loud hissing sound was followed by the announcement that the airlock was open.

Ryan looked down through the hatch. He saw a bank of red lights below, which must have been the warning signal that the outer hatch was open. He climbed through it, took hold of a ladder and began descending to the next deck. Above his head, the hatch snapped shut, and he watched the wheel spin closed. He heard a clank as the bathyscaphe unhitched, and then the sound of its engines as it headed back to the station. Finally, the bank of lights over his head flashed from red to yellow.

"Senator Ryan," a soft voice called to him from below, "I hope your trip down here was a pleasant one?"

Mitchell Ryan continued down the ladder until both feet were firmly planted on the deck. "I'm afraid to admit that I'm not a very good passenger, Dr. Takahashi," he replied. "On the journey here from Earth, I opted for the deep freeze after that grueling slingshot around Mars. There was no way I was going to let them bounce me through the asteroid belt or put me through aerobraking around Jupiter without being completely out of it."

"That is most unfortunate," she said, a distant look in her eyes. Her porcelain-like features were cool, composed, even somewhat detached. "And how did the other members of your family enjoy the trip?"

Ryan cast a bewildered glance at her. "My two boys and their mother are still back on Earth," he said at last.

"What a pity that you are so very far from home and the ones you love."

"We felt it was best for them," he explained. "John's a junior at Penn State, and Tom's a sophomore at Maryland. I didn't see any reason to disrupt their schedule just to bring them here with me."

Yukiko Takahashi smiled slightly at the man's visible discomfort, then turned with little movement and started down the corridor. "My five year-old son Hiroshi and his paternal grandmother live with me on the Station," she volunteered. "Her presence keeps me humble. His presence reminds me the work that I am doing is for him and the generations that follow him, and not for me."

Ryan followed behind her. "Yes, of course, the work we're doing here is tremendously important for our children and the future of the Earth."

"And yet there are other children, whose silent voices cry out to be heard," she continued, without any emotion or intonation, "but their cries are not being heeded, are they, Senator Ryan?"

Mitchell Ryan sighed. He felt like he had just been expertly maneuvered into a fool's mate by a grandmaster chess player. "Dr. Takahashi, I've read your preliminary report, and thought far too much of it was speculative. I'm not interested in fantasy, just cold, hard facts that are thoroughly grounded in science. You've yet to produce a single shred of evidence that proves those 'creatures' are sentient, or that our mining operation will affect them in any way."

"I've been observing the Jovian lifeforms for nearly two years now, and their behavior suggests a higher level of consciousness."

"Where is the proof, doctor?"

Yukiko Takahashi paused for a moment, with her head bent in silent meditation, then turned to face the man straight on. "We have a rare opportunity here to study a completely different form of life," she said coldly, dispassionately, as if she was lecturing a graduate seminar at Princeton or New Tokyo in astro-biology. "All that we've ever known about life in the universe has been based on studying life on our own planet. But the simple, undeniable fact remains that every living creature, from the tiniest microbe to the most complex organism, is essentially the same on Earth. Humans and animals may appear to be physically different—particularly if you compare man with an elephant or a sperm whale—but we're all structured in the same way, from the same DNA. The discovery of an entirely new lifeform—not found on Earth—changes all that. We're no longer limited to studying just humans and animals; now we have a chance to look at life on another world," Yukiko continued. "These Jovian lifeforms are the product of millions of years of divergent evolution in a planetary environment quite different from our own. The vast differences that separate us from them—in terms of communication, technology and sociology—also reveal just how narrow-minded we are when it comes to accepting that which is not human. In fact, we may have to expand our limited definitions of what determines sentient life. Is it merely intelligence? Self realization? Are those humans who are mentally-challenged less sentient than those who are not? Perhaps there are no precise tests yet, no empirical proof that I can show you now, that will convince you otherwise. But we are dealing with something very special here."

"If they're sentient, then why haven't they contacted us all these years? We've been sending probes to Jupiter for more than a century," he said calmly, suppressing the urge to take her Ph.D. and shove it down her throat. "The probability that simple organisms would evolve into complex lifeforms on an inhospitable world like this, and that those complex lifeforms would then, in turn, gain sentience is highly unlikely. I see no evidence of an alien civilization. No cities or other structures. Whatever is down may well be, by your definition, sentient; but without something more concrete to go on, I'm afraid our mining operation will begin as planned."

"In New Japan, we are still raised to respect all life as sacred, from the smallest insect to the largest ocean mammal," she reported.

"Yes, I am aware of your many customs and rituals, and I don't have a problem with any of them. I'd actually welcome the chance to negotiate the mining rights to their planet with these creatures, but so far not one of them has come forward to bargain. They're like ants rushing about moving dirt from one place to another."

"Ants do serve a purpose."

"True, but whose?" Mitchell Ryan asked. "Certainly not their own since they don't accomplish anything to help themselves. Years and years of evolution, and they're still nothing but ants."

"Are human beings any better?"

Ryan disagreed with her, but he knew this interchange of views would amount to nothing. "It's a good thing there are practical people like me around," he boasted, trying to turn the discussion around, "otherwise, if we left things in the hands of the scientists, there'd be no progress at all."

"Progress? Do you call this progress, Senator? We have used up all of the natural resources of our own world, and now must mine those resources on other worlds. What happens when we have used up all the resources in the solar system? What then? Humanity goes onto the next star, and overmines that system as well?"

"That's the third time you've called me senator," he observed. "I resigned my seat in Congress over a year ago to take this post."

"I beg your humble pardon. I was mistaken," she said, without conviction. "I suppose the title of governor would be more appropriate."

The former senator shook his head. "No, I'm afraid that's not approved yet either. And until the Jupiter colony is officially recognized as a territory of the United States, I'd prefer you simply use the title of chief administrator."

Yukiko Takahashi paused again. She ran a delicate hand through her short black hair, and Ryan noted that was the first involuntary action she had made since his arrival. The woman said finally, "You seem reluctant to discuss the possible ecological threat your strip mining poses to the Jovian lifeforms."

"You know as well as I do, Doctor, how important these resources are to our families back home," he replied. "The liquid metallic hydrogen alone, in small quantities, is enough to satisfy the energy requirements of a major city on the Earth for nearly a year. The other gases provide the raw fuel for transportation, commerce and industry." Mitchell shrugged his shoulders, and put his hands in the air. "I wish there was some other way, but we simply don't have any choice in the matter."

"A matter of this importance surely deserves much more than a footnote in some planetary survey," she returned. "For instance, if your mining operation does threaten to destroy the ecological balance of the planet, we must have a contingency plan to preserve some of the natural habitat for the Jovian lifeforms. Otherwise, they may well be headed for extinction."

"Over a century ago, on Earth, certain environmental groups tried to stop loggers in the Pacific Northwest of the United States from cutting down timber in order to save the spotted owl from extinction," Ryan said, as he glared at the Japanese professor. "They chained themselves to trees, blocked roads and destroyed equipment; when that proved ineffective, they began killing the loggers and the federal deputies who had been called upon to restore the peace. Their actions not only cost the logging companies millions of dollars in revenue but also led to the loss of life— all in the name of one endangered species of bird that ultimately disappeared on its own. I'm not going to let that happen here."

"I never meant to suggest . . ."

"The company has agreed to fund your research through the end of the century provided you tender a report which is favorable to the operation."

Yukiko Takahashi was gravely silent.

Mitchell Ryan glanced at his Rolex watch, verified the time, then looked back at her. "My appointment as the Station's chief administrator becomes effective on Wednesday at noon, so I'll expect your final report no later than Thursday morning. That leaves you just about two days to come up with something more definite on those creatures of yours for the survey. If the report is not on my desk by Thursday, I'll expect your resignation in its place. Do I make myself clear?"

Dr. Takahashi nodded that she understood.

"Now, if you don't mind, I'd like to continue my tour of the Platform," he said, shoving past her in the narrow corridor. "I still haven't seen the forward observation chamber, and that was foremost on my agenda."

*   *   *   *   *

The forward observation chamber was only thirty-five feet across, and its interior seemed uncomfortably close to Ryan. Inside the oblong, double-walled compartment, he tried to imagine what working conditions would be like for the five technicians and three miners he had chosen for the project. The quarters were definitely tight, and as Mitchell Ryan surveyed the room, he couldn't think of a single item they could do without. Most of the equipment and instruments they would need for the actual drilling and mining process had been built right into the bulkhead. The chamber also contained cooking, washing, and toilet facilities, a first aid station, and a bank of video screens which would monitor the Platform's exterior views.

Ryan was not surprised by the lack of pressure suits or escape pods. The least rupture in the Platform's outer hull would spell instant death. They'd never survive in a suit or have time enough to climb into a escape pod as the outside pressure would crush them instantly. Thank goodness, he thought, the likelihood of such an occurrence was extremely rare, what with the Platform's various backup systems and redundancy plans.

The former senator was next drawn to the chamber's most distinctive feature, a ten-foot wide circular window. Constructed of a high-impact plexiglass, it overlooked the stormy surface of Jupiter. His pulse quickened as he craned forward for a better view.

"So, where are these so-called Jovian lifeforms of yours?" he asked, cupping his hands to the glass and staring out the window.

"I have been scanning the horizon for over an hour, but I can find no sign of them," a man replied, while slipping through the airlock hatch behind them.

"Mr. Ryan, this is my assistant Masaki Shibata."

Mitchell Ryan turned to regard him. Shibata was tall for an Asian male, and his youthful appearance belied his forty-five years—the last ten of which he had spent as Dr. Takahashi's assistant.

"*Konnichi wa*, Ryan-*san*," he said, first bowing and then shaking hands firmly. "I have been looking forward to meeting you."

"*Konnichi wa*," Ryan returned the greeting, with a respectful bow. He then asked how the scientist was doing, "*Ikaga desu ka?*"

"*Okagasama de genki desu*, Ryan-*san*," he replied warmly, explaining that he was very well. "*Anata wa?*"

"*Hai!*" Ryan affirmed.

"Do you speak Japanese?" Yukiko asked, attempting to mask her surprise at his perfect pronunciation with an innocent question. Her disguise was not entirely effective for Ryan saw right through it.

"No, not really. Only a few words and phrases," he responded with a modest shrug. "But I didn't come here to practice my language skills." The former senator groaned inwardly. He was sorry to sound so gruff, but he was working against a deadline of his own. "Dr. Shibata, I want to know the reason why, after all these months, you and Takahashi haven't been able to compile enough empirical evidence to support the claims these creatures are sentient."

"The Jovian lifeforms are very ellusive," he explained. "They start to approach the Platform, then break off for no apparent reason." Masaki paused for a moment of reflection, then continued, "In the last few weeks one of them, in particular, has come very close to the window on several occasions. If I did not know any better, I would say that 'he' has been very curious—"

"Curious," Ryan repeated, interrupting him. "That's a human emotion, Doctor. Are you trying to assign them human characteristics?"

"I can think of no other way to describe the behavior," Masaki confessed.

Mitchell Ryan shook his head. "And you agree with his assessment, Doctor Takahashi?"

"Yes, I do," she replied.

"Well, then, you've got just two days to make a believer out of me," Ryan said, turning to each of them and pointing at his watch. "Remember, that's all the time that you have left."

*   *   *   *   *

Half an hour later the pilot announced, "We're making our final approach to the Station. Please check your safety belts."

Mitchell Ryan complied, and pulled the belt tight over his shoulder and across his lap. He then nodded at the pilot who did not seem as friendly or as talkative as the other. She remained distant as she maneuvered the craft into place by firing the retro rockets.

A few minutes later he caught a glimpse of the Station, its polished metal surface shimmering with glints of yellow and red from the relatively dim star that crept over Jupiter's horizon. At nearly three-hundred yards in diameter, the massive structure seemed to float in the upper cloud stratum. Its central axis—supported from below by a nuclear reactor and connected by a long, narrow cone—rotated with a slight tilt through the billowing sea of clouds that swirled up from the planet. The rising towers and spires that dotted the Station's upper half reached toward space.

When they were less than a few yards away, Ryan watched through the porthole as the docking arms extended toward the small craft. He felt a slight jolt as they took hold, then listened for the familiar sound of metal clanging against metal. Within moments, the bathyscaphe was secure, the airlock was open, and a man wearing an orange fatigue was helping Ryan climb out.

The former senator closed his eyes, and took a deep breath, drinking in the rich oxygen. How strange it was to be breathing real air again.

"*Haha! Haha!*"

Ryan started. He whirled around to see who was crying out "Mommy" in Japanese. A little boy pushed through a handful of dockworkers, and raced by him, headed for the airlock, shouting "*Okasan-wa?*"—the equivalent of "Where's my Mommy?" in his native tongue. He guessed the child was Dr. Takahashi's son, and wondered if the boy had come down to the dock to meet his mother.

"*Dochira-sama desho ka?*" Ryan asked the boy his name, reaching back into his memory for the few Japanese phrases he had learned in college.

"Hiroshi," the little boy replied, crying.

"*Ah*, Hiroshi-*san*," he repeated gently. Ryan crouched down on one knee so he could look straight into the child's tear-filled eyes and put a consoling hand on his shoulder. "*Watashi wa* Mitchell Ryan."

The boy blinked, unfamiliar with the name.

"Do shita n desu ka?" Ryan asked.

At his request, Hiroshi told him exactly what was wrong. Even though Ryan was only able to follow bits and pieces with his limited Japanese vocabulary, he learned that the child had been frightened by strange images that appeared on his bedroom wall. He tried reassuring the little boy that everything would be all right, that he was probably just dreaming and that dreams could not hurt him. Ryan even offered to put him into contact with his mother through the Platform's comlink, but the boy just looked at him with big questioning eyes.

"Wakarimasu ka?" Ryan asked, hoping he understood.

"Domo arigato," Hiroshi said, thanking him with a bow.

Mitchell Ryan stood up again, and started to say, "Now, let's go find your grandmother," but before all the words could be fully spoken, the little boy ran away down the long docking bay. Impulsively Ryan made a motion to go after him, then thought better of it. If the boy had found his way down here, then he should be able to find his way back home, the former senator reasoned. The last thing he wanted to do was disrupt Station security with a report about a runaway child.

"What was that all about?" a voice demanded from one of the darkened recesses of the bay.

"Bad dreams," he groaned, feeling a sudden chill, "just like the one I'm having now." Ryan's attention was drawn into the shadows to a familiar figure. "Didn't I tell you I never wanted to see your face again?"

A sixty-year-old man emerged from the darkness. "Now, what kind of gratitude is that for the man who made you what you are today?"

"Reinhardt, I'm through paying my debt to you," he replied, "and those you represent."

Abruptly turning his back on him, Mitchell Ryan strode into the quiet corridor that connected the docking bay with the command center. His destination was the administrative offices, where his incompetent aide was probably waiting for him with a handful of trivial concerns. He was not about to stop walking.

"Ryan!" Reinhardt shouted, following after him. "You're not

through until we say you're through!"

Coolly, he stopped and turned around. "What do you want from me?"

Edward Reinhardt grinned. "The mining platform," he said in reply. He watched momentarily as Ryan squirmed at the mention of his pet project, then added, "Some of the corporate investors are very nervous. They're worried that the Platform won't be fully operational on Monday, what with all that talk of a strike and rumors of some kind of ecological protest. They're afraid they might actually loose money on their investment."

"You can assure them that I've got everything under control."

"That's not what I heard," Reinhardt remarked. "I heard you were having a problem with one of the project's scientists."

"Nothing that I can't deal with."

Reinhardt pulled him discreetly to one side. He then glanced back and forth, carefully surveying the corridor for other listeners. When he was satisfied they were alone, he looked at Ryan. "Takahashi is a liability," he said bluntly.

Incredulous, Mitchell Ryan shook his head. "She's just a damned idealist, that's all. She doesn't pose any real threat to the project. I can handle her."

"You don't seem to realize-she's already a threat," he insisted under no uncertain terms. "Her preliminary report has already raised certain concerns among environmental groups. There's even talk in Congress of a special commission to look into her allegations that the mining operation will threaten a new, and potentially friendly, lifeform. Her continued presence on the Platform just makes matters worse. Takahashi must be discredited, and silenced permanently."

"I said I could handle her."

"I'm afraid that's no longer an option."

"What are you going to do? Throw her out of an airlock without a pressure suit?"

"Well, that's entirely up to you, isn't it?"

"Up to me?" Ryan demanded, suspecting his words had somehow been misunderstood. "What the hell's that supposed to mean? What's up to me?"

"I don't care how you handle it," he replied "Just do it quietly."

Edward Reinhardt's eyes narrowed, his gaze judging him with a look he knew well. For an instant Ryan wanted to think this was some kind of practical joke; but then, as he examined the gaze more carefully, he realized that Reinhardt meant business.

"Don't give me that look," he said firmly. "I'm not one of your cold-blooded assassins." Ryan pushed him away with both hands. "You may think that just because you bought me a few elections and got me seats on a couple of key Congressional committees that you own me. But I've long since paid that debt. I'm my own man now, and I alone decide what's in my best interests."

Reinhardt appeared mildly annoyed. "That's becoming increasingly apparent."

"I want nothing to do with your dirty deals, and I'll not stand by and watch you murder an innocent woman."

"You seem to act as if you had some choice in the matter," he concluded, turning away from Ryan and hurrying down the corridor.

Mitchell Ryan pounded his fist in anger. Long ago he had promised himself that, if he ever managed to wriggle free of Reinhardt and men like Reinhardt, he'd never again do anything questionable. He felt that he had managed to achieve that by resigning his Congressional seat and accepting the appointment to the Station. Little did he realize at the time, what was fast becoming apparent to him now. He had simply changed one venue for another where the stakes were even higher than before.

Ryan walked over to one of the Station's many comlinks, and dialed security. "Hello, this is Mitchell Ryan," he said into the microphone. He paused for a moment, trying to think of what to say, then surprised himself. "A little Asian boy, approximately five years old, just ran out of the docking bay. His name is Hiroshi Takahashi. Without scaring him, could you see that he gets back to his quarters? Thanks, I owe you one."

*   *   *   *   *

Yukiko Takahashi stood alone at the great circular window of the foreward observation chamber, her petite Asian form dwarfed by the vast ocean of dense gas and floating clouds. She watched as several Jovian lifeforms broke through the clouds over an atmospheric storm system and propelled themselves carelessly across the sky; she even recognized the one Masaki had nicknamed Cloud Dancer for its distinctive locomotion. But as she stretched her arms out against the glass to embrace them, they began moving away, out of her field of vision.

Tears were in her eyes, and starting to roll down her cheeks as their silhouettes faded into the distance. Her vision blurred, and she angrily swiped her forearm across her face. The smear of teardrops glistened beneath the fine, dark hairs of her arm, changing color with the red and brown hues of Jupiter.

Desperately, Yukiko pressed her hands against the cold glass, shielding her eyes to peer deeper into the clouded sea, but the lifeforms were no longer there.

She heard footsteps, and turned, still crying.

Her assistant Masaki Shibata stood in the entrance to the chamber. "Mr Ryan has returned to the Station," he reported in Japanese.

She stared at him with complete incomprehension.

"You wanted me to let you know—"

"Yes, yes, I remember," she replied, biting her lower lip to keep it from trembling. "Now, please leave me alone."

"Kiko-*san*, what's wrong? Why are you crying? Did I say something that upset you?" he asked, moving to her side. Shibata tried to show that he understood what she was feeling by putting his arm around her, but Takahashi shrugged him off.

Unblinking, she stared back out the window.

"I want to know what's going on," he insisted. "Please tell me what's wrong."

Yukiko felt confused, agitated, embarrassed—a hundred different things all at once. But her sense of dignity prevailed. "I just want to be alone for a while," she replied, again drying her eyes with her forearm. "Thank you for your concern."

"Concern," Shibata repeated the word like a man who had just been mortally wounded. "I thought we were closer than that, but maybe I was wrong."

"Oh, Masaki!" she cried, and burst into tears once more. She then turned, and buried herself in his embrace. "Please . . . no questions. I do not want to talk. Just hold me."

Masaki Shibata just held her.

*   *   *   *   *

At noon on Wednesday, a crowd of one hundred and fifty people was waiting for Mitchell Ryan in the recreation hall, and everyone rose politely, clapping, as he entered behind his administrative aide. Flashbulbs exploded in his face, and reporters from several networks struggled in vain to have a brief word with him. But as he strolled by, Ryan simply smiled and nodded at their familiar faces. He then whispered to his aide: "Charlie, I thought I told you I wanted to keep this small."

Charles Bradford shrugged. "Once the media was involved, I didn't have much choice."

The former senator waved once at the crowd, then sat down in the front row, while his aide climbed several steps to the podium. Everyone returned to his seat, and the recreation hall fell silent, except for the occasional cough or whisper. In the very back of the room, Edward Reinhardt stood in the shadows, waiting.

"Ladies and gentlemen," Bradford spoke into the microphone, "It gives me great pleasure to introduce the three-time Congressman and twice-elected Senator from the great state of Maryland, Mitchell Ryan."

As Ryan ascended the rostrum amidst another round of applause, he seized the opportunity to shake several hands of those nearest the stage. He then waved again at the crowd, and took his place at the podium. "Distinguished guests, ladies and gentlemen, members of the press," he began his speech, "I want to thank you for the warm show of support you've given me during this very difficult and trying transition.

"My predecessor was a tireless and dedicated public servant, and a very capable administrator. His untimely death has left a tremendous void in the community which he was such a vital element. And he will most assuredly be missed. Therefore, it was with some reluctance and a deep sense of duty that I decided to resign my seat in Congress to assume his position as chief administrator. Although I can never begin to fill his shoes, I want you to know that I will do everything within my power to see that his dreams for this Station all come to pass."

The recreation hall resounded with applause, and Ryan used the moment to whisper a sincere thanks to his aide for setting the whole thing up.

"Some years ago, when I entered the public arena, I wanted to make a real difference for my country. To not only have the voice of my constituency heard on the floor of Congress but also to pass legislation that would make the lives of everyone somehow better. I tried to do just that, and over the years, the people of Maryland gave me their vote of confidence by returning me to the House several times and electing me to the Senate twice," he stated simply but elegantly. "Now I have been asked to undertake a new and challenging role. Though I would have preferred to continue serving the people of the United States, I realize that it is better to put aside my own personal interests for those that would better serve the planet as a whole . . ."

While the former senator dazzled his audience with his familiar political rhetoric, Masaki Shibata was choking to death several hundred kilometers below the Station. Someone had deliberately reversed the oxygen and nitrogen mixture in the forward observation chamber. The oxygen-rich air might not have proved fatal in any other environment, but under the tremendous pressure needed to maintain life support on the mining platform, the gas was far more lethal than cyanide. Once he had started breathing it, the highly corrosive gas began burning away the inner lining of his lungs. In a matter of minutes, Shibata was literally drowning in his own lung tissue . . .

"With the big task ahead, we have to take even bigger chances," Ryan continued. "Franklin Delano Roosevelt once said that we should put a higher premium on trying new ideas to old problems rather than just relying on the way that things have always been done. That solutions were more important than simply doing the right thing all the time." He glanced down at his notes, cleared his throat, and looked up again. "We've been given an important task by the people of the Earth, and they're counting on us to see that task through. We have a responsibility to try everything within our power to solve their resource problems, and keep trying until those problems no longer exist. And with your help, we will succeed.

"I would just like to thank all of you for coming," he concluded over the sound of unanimous applause, "and God Bless you in the months ahead."

As he made his way from the podium, Ryan exchanged the usual small talk and pleasantries that courtesy demanded in situations like this. He smiled, and nodded, and repeated "Hello, nice of you to come" in a well-rehearsed, cordial manner. But before Bradford could usher him from the room, several reporters were demanding impromptu interviews with the new chief administrator. Mitchell Ryan obliged, and spoke at length with the press about his goals for station, always mindful of questions that required answers not part of his standard repertoire.

Finally, the crowd in the recreation hall dispersed, and the members of the media had run out of questions to ask the former senator. Ryan felt wrung out. He glanced around, looking for an escape, and found himself face to face with Reinhardt.

"Congratulations," he offered, extending his right hand, "that was a most inspiring speech."

"What are you doing here?" Ryan demanded.

Edward Reinhardt looked astonished that the new station administrator did not know. "Mitchell," he said in protest, "I came down to hear your speech, of course."

"Cut the crap. What are you really doing here?"

Reinhardt leaned toward him, and whispered, "I've taken care of your problem."

"Right now, my only problem is you," he scowled, trying and failing to maintain an outward appearance of civility for whomever might still be lingering about the hall. "Get the hell out of here!"

Reinhardt backed off, startled. The sixty-year-old man stormed away without a backward glance, muttering something about gratitude and thanks.

Less than a hour later, Mitchell Ryan understood exactly what he meant by "problem."

"There's a dead man at my mining site," Ryan shouted, barging into the elegant, exclusive presidential suite that overlooked the Station's central core, "and that makes me very angry."

Edward Reinhardt stepped out of the toilet facility, a straight razor in his left hand and shaving cream partially covering the right side of his face. "Come in," he said with a frown. "I guess I should have someone come up and check that lock. I wouldn't want to have just anyone barging in here."

"I said there's a dead man at—"

"Yes, yes, I heard you," he replied, returning to the marble basin in the adjoining room. "Shibata—that was an unfortunate accident. Takahashi was the real target."

"Unfortunate," Ryan repeated. He followed after the old man, determined to have it out with him, once and for all. "Is that all you got to say? Unfortunate. We're not talking about some dumb animal that ran out in front of a speeding truck."

Reinhardt continued shaving, moving the razor across his face with slow, determined strokes. When he finished, the sixty year-old reached into the basin, and splashed a handful of water into his face. He then straightened up as far as he could, revealing a stiffness in his back, and reached for a plush red towel.

Ryan's eyes narrowed as he studied the other man's wrinkled features. They were cool and unflappable. "This doesn't seem to bother you."

"No, Mitch, it doesn't bother me," he said, wiping his face once with the towel then throwing it carelessly across the room. "What does bother me is your reaction to it."

"Am I supposed to be grateful?"

"For a start," Reinhardt returned.

Mitchell Ryan shook his head. He seemed at a complete loss for words, not that it mattered. He felt like nothing he said made a difference.

He hurried across the room, opened the sliding glass door and stepped onto the balcony for a breath of fresh air. "Did I just fall through the looking glass?" Ryan asked, his voice full of irony. "Aren't you the guy who used to tell me that one of the things that separated us from the dictators and tyrants of the world was the value we placed on human life?"

"Yes, that was theory," he answered with a slight shrug. "But this is fact. And the fact is that what we are doing here is a very important and necessary part of our efforts to maintain our way of life. Reality, Mitch, is often very different from theory."

Ryan leaned over the suite's narrow balcony to take in the cycloramic view of the Station's central core. The sight was breaktaking, even to someone who had just staredinto the great eye of Jupiter. He watched the hang-gliders weaving back and forth, then looked down to see people the size of ants moving along various ramps and platforms far beneath him. The warm air from the reactor below swept against his face, and, for a moment, Ryan forgot where he was. But only for a moment.

"I take that back," he said, putting his thumb close to one eye and squinting to remove one of the people below from his line of sight. "Shibata wasn't some dumb animal to you. He was an ant, and you stuck your thumb out and squashed him."

Reinhardt carefully hid his smile, and managed a look of disdain instead. "You seem to have a gift for the fanciful this evening."

Ryan drew himself together, and the determined look settled back on his face. "Now, I want to show you something," he said, returning to the room and putting a hand under the other man's elbow. Mitchell tugged firmly on Reinhardt's arm, and the sixty year-old reluctantly accompanied him to the balcony. "I want to show you what the view is like from way up here."

"I don't like views."

"Really," he commented, forcing him to the edge.

"I'm not comfortable with heights," Reinhardt said, struggling to break free.

Ryan maintained his grasp, and pressed the old man's upper body to the railing. "Well, then, by all means you should take a look."

"Mitchell, have you lost your mind!" he shouted.

"I could throw you over this railing just as easily as you killed Shibata," he scowled, pushing him closer to his doom. "But I didn't take this post to become partners with you in murder."

Reinhardt's legs began to buckle, and his breathing was hard and labored.

"And this is never going to happen again," Ryan added. "Right?"

Edward Reinhardt was gravely silent.

"Am I right?" Ryan demanded an answer. When he realized that he wasn't going to get one, he simply loosened his grip, and stepped aside.

Reinhardt scrambled backwards until he reached the safety of his room, and collapsed to the floor, clutching his chest. His breathing continued to be hard and labored, and sweat was dripping from his forehead. The wrinkles on his face had flattened out into a frightful death's-head. But he still managed the smile of a man who just stared down the grim reaper, and had lived to boast about it.

"No more murders, no more accidents," Ryan explained. "Or you'll be the next one they find dead." Mitchell Ryan then turned and walked out into the illuminated hall. He hoped he had made his message clear to Reinhardt. He wasn't a killer, but if pressed, he felt like he was capable of anything.

*　*　*　*　*

Rumors of Masaki Shibata's death had spread through the Station like wildfire, but the only truth lay in the official coroner's report on Ryan's desk.

The chief administrator pushed the report away and sat back watching the steam rise from his hot cup. He debated whether he should drink his morning's worth of caffeina or simply inject it into his veins. The milky-white alkaloid had replaced coffee as a stimulant because of the Station's embargo on goods imported from South America, but had not improved on the flavor. It still tasted bitter to him. Ryan took a couple of sips, frowned, and then pulled the autopsy report back to him. He had already been up for over twenty-six hours, and had the suspicious feeling that it was going to be another one of those days.

A sudden commotion in his outer office confirmed that suspicion. "Charlie, what the hell is going on out there?" he shouted at the door.

"Wait a minute! You can't go barging in there," Ryan heard his administrative aide cry out from the other side of the door, and all at once both Bradford and Dr. Yukiko Takahashi were standing in front of his desk.

"I'm sorry, Mr. Ryan," Charles Bradford apologized, his face beet red. "I told her you were busy. She just kinda got by me."

"Thanks a lot, Charlie," Ryan groaned. "If I need any more of your help, I'll call."

"Yes, Mr. Ryan," Bradford replied, turning and closing the door behind him.

"*Ya, genki kai?*" Ryan greeted her in Japanese. "Have you come to deliver your report to me personally? You could have simply filed it electronically.?"

Yukiko Takahashi half smiled, an expression devoid of amusement or goodwill. The woman's lips were trembling, and her hands were shaking so bad that she had to take hold of the corner of his desk to keep them steady. She looked down the length of the desk, and now Yukiko did grin when she saw the coroner's report in his hands.

"I know you killed Masaki," she said with a distinct lisp, the words tumbling out of her mouth in an almost unintelligible manner.

"Now, hold it right there," Ryan objected. "If you're going to insult me—"

"You are the one who insults me with your lies," Yukiko rambled on, impatiently stepping over his objections. "You have no honor."

"I didn't kill anyone, Yukiko."

"Then his murder was committed under your orders."

"You can't really believe that."

"Yes, I do."

"What reason would I have to kill your assistant?" Ryan appealed to the scientist's rational side. He then cleared his throat, straightened his shoulders and sat forward in his chair. The Station's chief administrator did not need any more stress, and yet, as he examined the woman's movements more closely, he sensed that there was something terribly wrong with her.

"I am very sorry that he's gone, but I can assure you that I had nothing to do with his death," he continued by passing her the official autopsy report. "According to this report, the coroner has determined the cause of Masaki's death as accidental. He could find no evidence of foul play on the body or at the site."

Yukiko Takahashi did not bother to examine the report. She crumpled the papers into a ball in her fist, and shook it at him. "This means nothing," she uttered. "You and I both know it is a lie."

"And how would I know that?"

"Because you have no honor."

Mitchell Ryan rose from his chair. Takahashi wasn't the only one in the room who was out of patience. "I've heard just about enough out of you, doctor," he shouted. "And I've wasted just about all the time I'm going to with this paranoid delusion of yours. Thank you very much. That will be all!"

"That's not all!" She stood and glared at him. "Not until I get to the bottom of this. If you didn't kill him, then someone else did." Shaking with frustration, and no longer able to control the tremors in her arms and legs, Takahashi turned to leave the room. As she did so, her eyes fastened on a picture of Ryan and two handsome young men. The proud father and his sons, she thought, her mind shifting to thoughts of her own son Hiroshi. She took another step, and stumbled, catching the toe of her right foot on the heal of her left, like a drunkard failing to walk a straight line.

Ryan shook his head, and sighed. For the last few minutes he had been trying to figure out what was wrong with her. Just then, he knew. She had all the tell-tale signs of High Pressure Nervous Syndrome—disorientation, tremors, nervousness, paranoia.

He came out from behind his desk and caught her at the door. "I think you better go back to your quarters and get some rest, doctor," he said, his bulky American frame looming over the petite Asian woman.

"I don't need any rest," she stuttered. "I've got a report to complete—"

"That report can wait until after you've gotten some rest."

"—and a killer to find."

Mitchell Ryan folded his arms across his chest, and stared directly into her eyes. "You're relieved, doctor. Don't make me fire you as well," he said. "Now go home, and get some rest. I don't want you going anywhere near the Platform until after you've had at least seventy-two hours topside."

"Yes, sir," Yukiko agreed. But she had no intention of obeying his orders, and returned immediately to the forward observation chamber.

*   *   *   *   *

Yukiko Takahashi was feeling desperate as she searched the clouds for some sign of the Jovian lifeforms. If she failed to make contact with them, then she brought dishonor down upon herself. The Japanese scientist glanced over her shoulder at the clock in the rear of the chamber, and realized she was quickly running out of time. She knew the mining operation would begin as planned on Monday, and feared what it might mean to them.

She sat with her legs crossed on the deck, her hands still shaking so badly that she took hold of her knees to steady them. She then closed her eyes, and tried to settle her thoughts. Takahashi had often dreamed of studying life on other planets since she was an undergraduate at Princeton, and her assignment to Jupiter was the answer to many years of dreaming. She felt more comfortable in orbit around the gas giant than any other place on Earth, even New Tokyo, where she had been born and raised in a very traditional household, and the United States, where she had been educated. Like most Japanese who studied aboard, she had been rejected by her own people, and made the object of suspicion by others. Even her own parents, who still bore thirty-year-old scars from the great trade wars, clung to many isolationist beliefs. They disapproved of her choice of schools, and refused to acknowledge her doctorate when she had completed her studies. Her decision to marry a shuttle pilot, and live on one of the off-world colonies, was made more of necessity than choice. Only Masaki and her husband knew the reason why she left Earth, and now one was dead, and the other no longer cared. Perhaps that was the reason why the Jovians meant so much to her. They had no preconceived notions about humans, as far as she could tell. They came near the

Platform with, what she perceived as, a wide-eyed innocence. And just like children, they needed her as protector and guardian.

Feeling a sudden sensation in her head, she opened her eyes to discover the room was spinning all around her. Yukiko tried to pull her body upright, but slumped to the floor, a mass of shakes and quivers.

*   *   *   *   *

Mitchell Ryan was trying to fight off an extreme case of mental fatigue by playing a round of virtual golf in the recreation center.

He walked onto the fourth tee, and teed up the Penfold Hearts—his ball of choice which he had programmed into the computer simulation. Off to the side, he took one or two careful, concentrated practice swings. He then took up his stance, addressing the ball straight on, and brought the head of his golf club back in a wide slow arc. With his eyes glued to the ball, he snapped his wrists and whipped the club head through. The ball soared about two hundred feet, paused elegantly in the air, then dropped down onto the fairway.

"Excellent shot," his caddie commented, the voice of the computer-generated image flat and lifeless.

Ryan nodded his head and smiled. He found few physical activities as stimulating and conversely relaxing as a good round of golf. Often, when he had been a Congressman and found himself overwhelmed with trivial committee work, he would sneak out to a favorite course just over the Potomac River in Virginia. Nothing quite relieved the stress of his political duties like the peaceful tranquility of that eighteen-hole course in Arlington. Today, he was shooting a smaller but more challenging course at Diamond Ridge in Baltimore; earlier in the week, he had played the Royal Saint Marks just outside London.

Of course, he knew that he wasn't really in Baltimore, and hadn't recently traveled to Great Britain, but the computer simulation made it appear virtually real to him. While the room was only slightly bigger than his office, projections on the four walls, ceiling and floor provided the illusion of a golf course that seemed to stretch out for miles in every direction. There was actually no fairway, no green, no tee and no Penfold Hearts—only the golf club that he was holding was real. The safety goggles he wore over his eyes responded to his thoughts, converted those thoughts into concrete images with the help of the computer, and made him appear to be shooting a tremendous game. If he had wanted to serve an ace at Wimbledon or hit a homerun out of the park at old Wrigley Field, all he had to do was program the simulation, carry through with the physical moves and imagine the sensation. Ryan preferred swinging at golf balls.

When he and his caddie reached the ball on the fairway, Ryan selected a nine iron from his set of American Ben Hogans to make his next shot. He addressed the ball, swung quickly, lifted his head and shanked the Penfold Hearts almost at a right angle. A foot of virtual turf flew up, but the ball went less than ten yards.

"You're slicing to the right," the voice of a shadow scolded him from the side. Ryan turned, and the vague shadow at the entrance to the recreation room gradually assumed the shape of Edward Reinhardt. "You never could make that shot with a nine iron."

Mitchell Ryan groaned. "Since when did you become such an expert?"

"I taught you everything you know," he said, selecting an iron from Ryan's golf bag and taking one or two careless practice swings.

"I guess that's the real reason why you have so little left," Ryan replied coldly. He slipped the nine iron back into his bag, and pulled a stitched leather cover over the club's wooden head. "You've not beaten once me in over twenty years."

"We've not played in twenty years," Reinhardt returned. "Not since you made such an ass of yourself at the Hampton invitational."

"The woman was cheating."

"So what!" the older man exclaimed. "Everybody cheats at something—cards, taxes, tests, relationships. It's a fact of life. She was just unlucky enough to get caught at it." He stared at Ryan with a soulless gaze. "Didn't you learn anything from me?"

"Too much," he quipped. "Particularly about cheating."

"Why must you always reduce everything down to its most

simple terms? Black or white, good or evil. Haven't you learned yet that there's more gray in the solar system than any other color?" Reinhardt asked. "After all, isn't this golf course just some elaborate computer program designed to cheat your mind and senses?"

Mitchell Ryan snapped off his goggles, stormed over to the emergency override switch and smashed it, breaking the safety mechanism with a single blow of his fist. Instantly the eighteen-hole illusion was gone. "No, it isn't," he defended. "This is a computer simulation, nothing more. What men, like you and me, do with it is what makes the program good or evil."

"Come, come now, Mitch. You mustn't be so bitter. I only had your best interests at heart."

Ryan relaxed his fist. The cutting edge was red and swollen, and he knew that it would soon show a bruise. "I suppose this is the part when you tell me how much like a son I've been to you."

Reinhardt started to reply, but was cut off before he could say a word.

"I guess you had my best interests at heart all along," he added with a grimace. "I let you sucker me into all those golf tournaments. I let you buy me all of those expensive gifts—the cars, the stock, the women. I accepted all of those special favors—the committee appointments, the trips to New Freedom, the tax variances—all because you had me convinced that it was in my best interest. Did it ever occur to you that I might grow to resent you for all of that?"

"Well, no, but I can see how that was a mistake."

"A very big mistake. But that's all in the past now. I don't want any more of your gifts or special favors, and I certainly don't want anything more to do with you."

Reinhardt grinned. "You can't just cut me out."

"Watch me."

"You can't just run away."

"Can't I?" Ryan smiled confidently. "I'm not running away. I'm right here, and I plan to stay right here. I'm just not your man anymore."

"But we're family—"

"Well," Ryan interrupted, "you may be a member of my political lobby in Washington and the grandfather of my two boys, but you are nothing to me." He seized the club out of the other man's arthritic hands, and shoved it into his golf bag. He then turned to leave. "When I divorced your daughter Helen, I divorced you and all of those clowns you work for."

"Divorces end marriages, Mitch, not partnerships. The two of us are joined for life."

"We are nothing. Get that!" Ryan held up his swollen hand with its thumb and forefinger locked into a circle, and thrust it into his face. "Zero. Zilch—nothing!"

Reinhardt staggered back, surprised. "How ironic," he mumbled after a moment of awkward silence. "I came here to offer you a gift."

"Didn't you just hear me? I don't want anything more from you."

"Well, then, let's just call it a peace offering."

The Station administrator paused at the door with his back to the other man, listening.

"That liability we spoke of," Reinhardt said. "I took care of it myself."

"Just like you took care of Shibata?"

Reinhardt acknowledged with a slight nod of his head.

Mitchell Ryan dropped his clubs, and scrambled to the only comlink in the room. "For your sake, Edward, she better be alive and breathing," he growled. "Now, where did you leave Takahashi?"

"The Platform," he said at last.

"Damn!" Ryan swore, typing the access number into the keyboard. He had warned her not to go near there.

"Don't bother," the old man retorted. "I already took the precaution of disabling the communications link to the Platform."

"You sonuvabitch, what else aren't you telling me?"

"Nothing—"

Ryan typed another sequence into the panel. "Charlie," he shouted into the comlink, "have a team of medics waiting for me in the docking bay!"

Reinhardt took a step toward the door, but Ryan saw him out of the corner of his eye. He grabbed the sixty-year-old man by the lapels of his designer jacket, spun him around and flung him to the center of the room. Edward Reinhardt hit the floor with a thud.

"You're not going anywhere," Ryan shouted, his voice echoing loudly off the four walls. "You're going to wait right here until I get back. And you better pray that she's still alive, because if she isn't, you're going to answer to me!"

He yanked the microphone out of the comlink, then flipped a switch on the computer simulation panel just outside the door. The room was suddenly transformed into a treacherous mountain range. Reinhardt lunged for the edge of a nearby cliff, and hung on for dear life.

"And to keep you occupied until I get back," he said, throwing the older man his goggles, "why don't you try some rock climbing on Mars."

Mitchell Ryan then locked and sealed the door.

* * * * *

Thirty minutes later, Ryan, the pilot and two medtechs were scrambling through the Platform, past the empty bunks in the aft compartment, through the central office complex and into the connecting corridor. They paused only long enough for Ryan to flood the room with a new air mixture, then continued through the heavy airlock door and into the forward observation chamber. He half expected to find Takahashi sprawled out on the deck with one hand around her throat and the other grasping for the comlink. That was the way they had found her assistant Shibata. But when they finally reached her, she was resting peacefully, like a sleeping princess in a fairy tale.

"Nitrogen asphyxia," the one technician said to the other, bending down on one knee and pressing two fingers against the side of her neck.

"She probably never knew what hit her," the other replied, turning to Ryan and the pilot. "The overpowering mixture of nitrogen gas just sort of crept up and carried her away . . ."

The first medtech glanced up from examining her, and shouted,

"Hey, I've got a pulse."

At once, the two men sprang into action. While one filled a syringe from a bottle of adrenaline, the other straddled the woman's upper torso, pumping her chest with his hands. He next locked his lips over hers, and started mouth-to-mouth resuscitation, using the same rhythm he had been pumping her chest. He continued breathing into her lungs for a few minutes, then climbed back on top of her body and resumed pumping her chest.

His partner instantly followed his lead. Once he had finished injecting her with the stimulant, the medtech pulled a small, lightweight respirator from his equipment pack. He then placed its black rubber mask over her mouth, and renewed attempts to restart her breathing by pumping a squeeze bag.

Ryan knelt beside her, at Yukiko's head, and gently stroked her short, black hair. As difficult as it was confronting her with his skepticism regarding the Jovian lifeforms, he had no real quarrel with Dr. Takahashi. In fact, he realized now that he liked and respected the Japanese scientist and believed her to be genuine—more than he could say for Reinhardt or the others. Takahashi had the conviction that she was right, and stuck with it in spite of overwhelming adversity. And even though they disagreed, he admired her for that conviction. Ryan just hoped they could bring her back.

"Come on, breathe!" the technician cried out, plying her with fresh air.

Yukiko Takahashi remained still.

"She's not responding. We're gonna lose her. Come on, dammit!" the other medtech swore at her, then pounded the woman's delicate chest.

"You're killing her!" Ryan shouted beside him, feeling the urge to do something—anything.

The pilot held him back. "No, they know what they're doing. Just let them work."

The medtech continued pounding on her chest.

"Come on, breathe!" his partner repeated.

Mitchell Ryan stared down into Takahashi's face; her porcelain features had gone ashen. Panicked, he looked at them and cried,

"Help her, dammit!"

Frantically the two technicians glanced at one another, then returned to their patient.

"Fight, goddammit—" one shouted, pumping hard and fast on her chest with the palms of his hands.

"—FIGHT!" the other completed.

Ryan reached out to the Japanese scientist and gently squeezed her hand. "You can't just die on me like this," he whispered in her ear. "The fate of the Jovians rests in that report of yours. They're counting on you to make their voices heard." He thought about his words for a moment, then added, "But they're not the only ones. I'm relying on your judgment to keep me honest."

Takahashi's eyelids flickered, her face twitched and her hands clenched and unclenched in spasm.

"Yukiko!" he cried, feeling a cool sensation of relief wash over his perspiring face.

Finally, with a feeble cough, Takahashi pushed the mask away from her face, and started to breathe on her own. She choked at first, struggling for each breath. But gradually, the Asian woman began to take the fresh air into her lungs with little difficulty. It seemed impossible that she was still alive, but Ryan was beginning to believe that nothing was impossible.

"*Domo arigato*," she said to him, with a slight nod of her head.

"*Dozo, nami-mo*," he replied modestly.

A few minutes later, Ryan helped the two medtechs carry Yukiko Takahashi through the adjoining rooms to the docking hatch. She was still feeling lightheaded, and could barely put one foot in front of the other. She probably needed a few hours in a decompression chamber, followed by two or three days of rest in sick bay.

When they reached the landing ladder, Ryan informed the others that he had decided to remain behind—using the excuse the bathyscaphe was designed as a four-man craft and might prove dangerous with five. He would simply wait for the next one. His gesture was certainly not a noble one, but no one suspected his motives. Ryan just wanted some time alone with his thoughts, and knew of no place on the Station, including his quarters, where he could be truly alone. Besides, he was still wondering what had kept her alive for so long without oxygen.

Ryan returned to the forward observation chamber, and looked out of the circular window.

At first he could only see the vast ocean of dense gas and floating clouds. Then an enormous shape, obscured partially by the clouds, floated up past the window and plunged back down toward the surface.

Mitchell Ryan gasped, awestruck.

None of the words or detailed drawings in Takahashi's report had even hinted at the sheer size or elegance of the creature. Ryan estimated it to be roughly one hundred feet in length, and though shaped like a hot-air balloon that was continually expanding and contracting, he likened the creature to a great blue whale. He watched as it rose toward the Platform, gathering small organisms and gas through a row of fringed plates in its mandible, much like a whale straining krill through its baleen. It glided up and past the window, all the while pumping its body up like some magnificent bodybuilder. Then, with several rhythmic contractions, the creature expelled both waste and gas from a rear exhaust, and went sailing into the clouds by jet propulsion. A moment later, hundreds of meters away, its majestic body--now slender and elongated—broke through the clouds. It floated for an instant on a warm updraft, then plunged back down to repeat the cycle again.

Ryan half expected such a tremendous creature to be clumsy and sluggish, but it moved like a graceful ballerina executing several leaps and turns in one, light flowing movement. Perhaps, he thought, this was the one they called Cloud-Dancer, for there was certainly a rhythmic quality to its locomotion.

As the creature again passed by the window, Ryan took particular note of its colorization and markings. He saw that Cloud-Dancer, while mostly biege in color, had several gray longitudinal furrows that ran along its streamlined body. And though its skin was smooth and hairless, he observed a row of small, stiff bristles near its crown. Neither of these features seemed to serve any purpose he could readily explain but they might be used in the future for identification purposes. He made a mental note to himself to tell that to Dr. Takahashi when she was fully conscious.

Cloud-Dancer was soon joined by a second one of its kind, and then a third. As they glided past the viewing window, Ryan had the strange sensation that he was being watched by them. Like he was the one on display, being observed and having his seemingly purposeless features recorded for some future identification. The thought sent his mind reeling.

He staggered back away from the window, and put the palms of both hands to his head.

Mitchell Ryan felt quite strange. He tried to shake off the feeling, dismissing his slight disorientation as the result of the high concentration of nitrogen gas that was still lingering in the chamber. The pilot of the *Montgolfier* had warned him about the effects of the gas, but at that moment he couldn't remember a damn thing she told him. His mind was suddenly spinning out of his head. He felt confused, light-headed, and it took every effort just to keep from losing his balance. But the more he struggled to maintain that balance, the more the dizziness intensified.

Ryan was losing control of himself. One moment, he could feel the muscles in his lower limbs tighten in response to a message sent from the brain to keep his legs from buckling, and the next, they were twitching and moving at commands that were not wholly his own. He fought the urge to fall, but eventually succumbed to a force that was far greater than his own. Ryan then attempted to roll over on his side, but discovered that he could not seem to move another muscle. Looking down at his right hand, he tried to focus on closing the fingers into a fist. But this simple task became an ordeal of unimaginable proportions as well. He struggled with each finger, but soon realized the futility of his actions. Ryan choked down a couple of breaths, his lungs laboring like a climber on Mt. Everest, then stared with unblinking eyes at the ceiling. He could no longer move on his own.

Within moments, the last ounce of feeling in his body had gone, and all that remained was a consciousness that seemed to drift in and out of reality. Ryan knew that he was laying helpless on the deck in the forward observation chamber, but his mind told him he was inching toward the edge of some great precipice. He struggled within himself to keep back, away from the edge, by trying to concentrate on things around him. First, he tried counting ceiling tiles, then he traced the outline of the florescent lightfixtures with his eyes. But his mind kept returning him to that damned precipice.

Finally, he simply gave in, and looked out into the dark abyss that lay before him. For all its unperceived depth, Ryan might well have been looking right into a black hole, or worse, the very bowels of hell. His mind screamed in horror at the thought. Then, as if in slow motion, he found himself plunging downward. Tumbling head over foot, he tried to grasp at something— anything that would break his fall—but his limbs did not respond. He just continued plummeting further and further into darkness.

. . . and at last, there is only darkness.

Then, as his eyes adjust, Ryan sees something, not clear at first, but something vague, formless. Gradually the image clears, and he observes a man bending down on one knee to comfort a child that is crying. He looks closer at the image, and sees himself reflected in the man. He is that man, or rather was that man, for he no longer feels connected to the image. Ryan is aware that he is viewing the image now as some distant third party. But he is doing more than just viewing the image; he is also experiencing the strong emotional feelings that were part of that moment. Feelings of fear and loss, love and hope overwhelm him, and lift him to another plane.

He becomes aware of something just beyond his grasp, and reaches out to touch it. Without warning, several hundred other images deluge his mind at once. They surge into his consciousness, and he tries assimilating each and every image as it unfolds. Ryan sees two friends holding each other in loving embrace . . . two adversaries arguing ethics . . . a small boy cowering in fear under his blankets . . . a crowd of people responding to a speaker with their applause . . . one man gloating, while another chokes to death alone. The images flood his senses with sounds and shapes, smells and tastes, thoughts and feelings that are all distinctly human. The sensations fill him to the point of bursting; then, with one mighty discharge, he releases them all.

Instantly he grows lighter, freer. Ryan is no longer human; he has exchanged his physical form with one of the lifeforms, and now soars above the Jovian clouds.

One moment, he floats above a warm updraft over the gas giant, and the next, he is dancing from cloud to cloud without a care in the world. Ryan tastes a familiar delight from childhood, and savors the intense feeling of living just for the moment. But as he turns his gaze toward the heavens and spies the first Voyager probe, his feeling of intense joy is quickly replaced by one of apprehension. Feelings of fear and loss, desperation and hopelessness wash over his new body, and begin to swallow him whole. Even though he still retains the instincts of his alien host to float, Ryan's human thoughts struggle to keep him aloft. But the harder he tries on his own, the deeper he sinks.

A Jovian voice whispers an incredibly powerful, yet simple command for him to "relax." He does not hear the message with ears, but rather with his entire physical being. Ryan is no longer afraid. The peace and absolute tranquility of the creature's thoughts gradually fill him with a sense of friendship and good will.

He stops struggling and is, at once, supported and sustained by several fellow lifeforms. They lift him up toward the heavens, rocking him gently. The sensation is pleasant, nurturing, and he grows lighter in their loving embrace. He feels he could stay here forever. After a passage of time, he is again soaring high above the clouds. Ryan savors the moment, drinking in the pure and simple joy of being, for he knows he must soon resume his human form. And with that thought, he is again human. He feels relaxed and at peace with himself, as if he had been sleeping for a long time and was now able to awake, refreshed . . .

. . . from a wonderful dream. Blinking as if awakening from a short nap, Ryan stared in absolute astonishment at the tiled ceiling of the forward observation chamber. He remembered everything quite clearly.

He looked down at his arms and legs, and felt life coursing back into his veins. He focused on his right hand, and ordered his fingers to close into a fist. They answered without hesitation. He then rolled onto his side and glanced up at the circular window, his gaze coming to rest on the alien lifeform that was hovering just outside the window. Recognition did wonders for his condition. A sudden remembrance shot a mega-dose of adrenaline into his system, and made his pulse quicken. But he knew there was nothing to fear.

Ryan reached toward the creature, slowly enough so that his actions would not be mistaken as hostile. Cloud-Dancer hung motionless. He put both hands on the glass, and felt vibrations on its cool surface. Feelings of good will and friendship seemed to radiate from the Jovian lifeform right through the window.

He stared at the creature for a long while, then opened his mouth to speak, but nothing came out.

Mitchell Ryan's mind had gone blank. What do I say, he thought, his eyes traveling up and down the length of the creature's body. The former senator felt disappointed in himself. He had never been at a loss for words throughout his entire political career; but now, at the very moment of contact with a completely new species, he couldn't think of anything to say.

"Hello, how are you doing?" he said haltingly, tripping over each syllable. "My name is—" Ryan stopped, mortified by his assumption the Jovians could speak English. He stared back at the creature, wondering how he was supposed to communicate directly with it.

Almost at once, he knew. Just as humans communicated with one another through words, they communicated through images. Not random images, he reasoned, but rather with images that conveyed some kind of emotional response. At first, their images must have been simple ones to convey the simple joy of being; but as the Jovian lifeforms began encountering the first human explorers and engineers, they incorporated these new images to communicate their strong emotional reactions. He suspected their first glimpse of an Earth probe must have become a universal image for fear and apprehension. Other images, like his encounter with Hiroshi in the docking bay or his argument with Reinhardt, also helped expand their "vocabulary" for the inevitable first contact with humans.

Nodding his head, Ryan turned away from the creature in embarrassment. He was the biggest fool in the world not to realize they couldn't communicate with him in a manner most humans found conventional. It was clear that he would have to adopt their unusual method of expression if he wanted to communicate with them.

He closed his eyes, cutting off all visual distractions from the outside, and focused on a familiar image in his mind that would convey greeting. He then ransacked his feelings for the single emotion connected with "hello." Initially, the creature did not respond to his message; but as Ryan struggled to perfect the image and get it right, Cloud-Dancer returned in kind.

For the next forty minutes, the two tried conversing, using simple images to convey even simpler thoughts. Common ground was established between them on the basis of failure rather than success. Cloud-Dancer had difficulty following the human's syntax, while Ryan found himself relying on the images he recalled from his waking dream rather than trying to create new ones. And each time the Jovian did respond favorably to a new image, Ryan's gentle snapshot was met with a barrage of images, most of which he could not even begin to understand.

Afterwards he was disappointed with his own limited imagination. He should have asked the Jovian questions about God, Creation, and life after death. But then he realized how difficult it would have been to make such abstract concepts clear. The one thing that was clear to him was that the Jovians had been trying to contact them all along, but he and the others had been either too stupid or too arrogant to notice.

He figured they probably began watching humans from a distance, waiting for just the right opportunity to make contact. Once the Station had been built and the Platform was nearing completion, one or two of them likely tried to communicate with humans. Apparently they may have even thought the scientists on the Platform were manifesting images in return, for they continued with their efforts. But the Jovian lifeforms probably mistook the human's cold, scientific probes as an exchange of some kind.

He could just imagine their frustration at trying to assimilate the probes, and failing to get a proper response. Ryan's own instructions to gather hard empirical data was ultimately what drove them away.

Only the strong emotions of life and death was what lured them back to the Platform.

Ryan stared back at the lifeform with unblinking eyes, and struggled to pull it all together neatly in his own mind. Even though they communicated in a uniquely separate way and were worlds apart ideologically, he somehow sensed the Jovians were more like humans than different. They may have actually needed one another more than either was willing to admit.

He nodded at the creature, which was still hovering beyond the window, and bid farewell when it was finally ready to move away.

*   *   *   *   *

Once Mitchell Ryan had returned to the Station, he had only one thought in mind—to find out how Yukiko Takahashi was doing. He climbed out of the bathyscaphe and quickly strode through the docking bay, forcing his administrative aide into a brisk jog just to keep up. As they moved down the corridor that connected with the central core, Charles Bradford rushed up to overtake his boss.

"Mr. Ryan," he said, "are you sure this is the right thing to do?"

"I don't understand what you mean," Ryan said.

"Postphoning the Platform's official opening on Monday, sir," he replied. Bradford seemed upset to Ryan, not agitated or angry, more anxious. "You could have a real public relations nightmare on your hand if there's any kind of delay."

Without turning his head, Ryan snarled, "I'm no longerconcerned with what the press has to say. But if you're that worried about it, draft a press release, and I'll look it over."

"What should I say?"

"I don't care," he responded, throwing his arms into the air. "You're supposed to be my administrative assistant. It's about time you started making executive decisions on your own."

"But what if I get it wrong?"

"Then you'll admit to your mistake, apologize and pray that

they trust you the next time."

"I'm not sure if I can do that, Mr. Ryan," Bradford confessed. "I'm not a very good liar."

Ryan's stride hesitated, but he kept going. "I'll issue a simple statement tomorrow," he conceded, with a deep sigh.

"And the unions?"

Mitchell Ryan strode on in silence.

"The unions will have to be told something," Bradford continued his litany of concerns. "They're not going to like being shut out on the first day of work. They'll expect to be fully compensated."

"I'll handle the unions."

Doggedly, Bradford followed Ryan through the heart of the central core. "I'm not sure that this is the right thing to do," he repeated. "Maybe you should take a moment to rethink this—"

Ryan swung around, grabbed Bradford by the lapels of his jacket, and shoved him against the bulkhead. "I know what I'm doing, Charlie," he snapped. "In fact, I've never been so sure in all of my life. The Jovians are sentient lifeforms, and they deserve the same considerations that we would extend any conscious being. If that means we have to negotiate with them for the rights to mine here, then we had better come up with an effective strategy."

Charles Bradford stared at him, visibly shocked by his boss's abrupt action. "I guess you know what this really means," he stammered.

"No, why don't you explain it to me."

"If you're wrong . . . we'll both be out of a job," he replied, forcing a laugh.

Ryan loosened his rigid grip on Bradford's lapels, and gradually lowered him to the deck. He then brushed out the wrinkles in his aide's jacket with the palms of both hands. He couldn't begin to explain what had just come over him, and made no effort to apologize.

"I guess you're probably right," he responded with a half smile, "but I'm not wrong."

Bradford nodded his head in agreement.

Mitchell Ryan turned to continue down the corridor, then glanced back at Bradford. "Oh, there is one thing that you can do for me, Charlie."

"Anything, sir."

"I want you to cancel Edward Reinhardt's visa," he said, as if the name meant nothing more to him than that of an anonymous passenger on a spaceship's manifest. "Then I want you to find him, and have him escorted off this Station immediately."

"Edward Reinhardt—" Bradford repeated the name with some familiarity.

Mitchell Ryan shot him a surpised look.

"—was found dead in recreation room five," Bradford continued. "Heart attack. We found his body sprawled over the emergency shutdown switch. And the panel was broken. Apparently, he must have been mountain climbing, using the advanced Mars program, became disoriented and tried to shut down the simulation. In his eagerness to stop the program, he must have broken the switch instead. Died right there on the spot without ever reaching the door."

Ryan paused for a moment of silence. He wasn't sure what he was supposed to feel. The news disturbed him greatly, and yet, at the same time, he couldn't help but feel a sense of release, much like a devoted servant who had just learned that his master was dead.

After another moment, he replied, "I'll see that his next of kin is notified."

"That's your prerogative, sir."

Ryan nodded. "If you need me, I'll be in sick bay," he said, as he turned away and left Bradford standing all alone in the corridor.

*　*　*　*　*

A nurse and two medical technicians were conferring in the Station's infirmary when Mitchell Ryan stepped through the door. Young Hiroshi Takahashi, who had been watching his mother with his face pressed up against the thick glass of the hyperbaric chamber, turned in anticipation of his approach. Ryan playfully mussed the boy's hair, and exhaled with relief at the site of Takahashi. Ryan knew that, despite the many tons of pressure in the chamber enclosing her, the Japanese scientist was finally out of danger and on the road to recovery.

Clad only in a bra and panties, Yukiko floated upright in a vertical position inside the chamber with a set of electrodes attached to key spots on her chest. The chief medical resident was attending her from the other side of the glass, aided by the two medtechs who had brought her back to life. He monitored her heartbeat and breathing, while the other two gradually increased the air pressure one atmosphere at a time. They hoped that by increasing the partial pressure of oxygen her blood would gradually be oxygenated. For a while it appeared as if she were trying to resist the urge to breathe normally, preferring short, irregular breaths instead. Then, with the site of Ryan, she relaxed, succumbing to the new air.

The chief resident turned away from the chamber, and angled his head toward Ryan. "Dr. Takahashi is responding well to the treatment," he reported without expression. "We should have her back to breathing at normal pressure in a couple of hours."

"Thanks, doc," Ryan said, smiling. "That's one I owe you and your staff."

The chief resident looked back at his beeping monitor.

Ryan pressed his face to the glass. He had not the slightest idea how the hyperbaric chamber worked, but he was convinced it could work miracles as he stared into the woman's face.

"*Ya, genki kai?*" Ryan asked her condition through the loud speaker.

Takahashi nodded that she was fine.

"Please accept my humble apology. You were right all along about the Jovians," he said, then repeated the words again in Japanese.

She shot Ryan a confused look that communicated more her surprise than confusion.

"It was truly amazing, and even now I'm having trouble believing that it actually happened—"

She continued to look at him, surprised.

"—but I won't bore you with the details. Suffice it to say, we both know that they are sentient beings," Ryan replied. "And just as soon as you're feeling better, I'm going to need your help to convince the others that what we experienced with the Jovians wasn't some nitrogen-induced hallucination—but real."

Yukiko Takahashi nodded and smiled.

*   *   *   *   *

Hundreds of kilometers away, in the updraft over an atmospheric storm system, Cloud-Dancer paused to absorb the image of her smile. It was warm and pleasant, and filled him with a sense of hope. All at once, the Jovian felt an impulse to play.

Swiftly, gracefully, with the perfect poise and composure of a ballerina, he soared back into the air. Cloud-Dancer glided upward, then curved his body so he broke over the crest of some upper-level clouds, and did a vertical flip and hurled back towards the surface. Carried away by the simple joy in the moment, he continued dancing from cloud to cloud until the Station was far behind him, somewhere in the vast obscurity of the heavens, where the dawn rolled on into night.

A Gift of Verse

Shirley Jackson's "The Lottery" and Ray Bradbury's "The Smile" are two of my favorite short stories; both present bleak depictions of the future in which mob rule and mass hysteria have replaced individual human rights and rationality. I didn't think either of those stories was relevant anymore in postmodern America until I tried to attend a showing of Martin Scorsese's "Last Temptation of Christ." I had to fight my way literally through picket lines of Fundamentalist Christians who were determined to keep me from seeing the film even though they themselves had not. In writing "A Gift of Verse," I wanted to explore those same themes, and found myself visiting a neighboring community of Jackson's and Bradbury's small town America.

They was goin' to town for a hangin'—she overheard her folks whisperin' to one another, and felt a sudden chill in her Sunday finest.

Seven year-old Martha Goodman covered her ears to the sound of thunder and peeked out from beneath several layers of tattered clothing. Even though dust particles and chunks of debris had long since filled the sky with a midnight shroud, the little girl often pretended she could feel the warmth of a distant sun. Today, she didn't feel much like pretending. She simply watched as darker clouds linked to form a vast canopy of thundershowers overhead, then shivered close to her brother in the back of their parent's horse-and-buggy as the cold, October rain began to fall.

Every Sabbath, her family would travel twelve perilous miles over the forgotten highway to Collinsville for Reverend Underwood's weekly sermon, then turn around and head back to their shelter. Twice a year, they would make a special trip for Michaelmas and Resurrection Day, and occasionally her father would ride into town for a meeting with the elders. But Martha had never known her parents to make such a fuss.

"Somethin' terrible's gonna happen," she whispered to herself, clutching tightly to her brother.

Once their buggy had reached the ruins of the small, Illinois town and her parents had gotten out to talk with friends, Martha looked up to her brother. "Why've we come to town, Josh? What are these folks doin' here all dressed up? It ain't Sunday."

"I reckon they's come here for the same reason we have," he replied, lifting her gently from the rear of the wooden carriage. "To take part in a hangin'. 'Paw' says it's our civic duty to punish all those who done brung us to this sorry state."

"Who's they fixin' to hang?" she whispered, with a nervous stammer.

"I hear told they's hangin' a real enemy of the people, today," Joshua reported to his sister in a low tone of voice. "A poet."

"What's a po-et?" she asked, stumbling on the unfamiliar, two-syllable word.

The twelve year-old boy did not glance down at her, but looked around the town square as people arrived in twos and threes. "A person who writes things that ain't true," he finally answered.

Martha screwed up her eyes. "Why's he do a dang fool thing like that?"

"I don't rightly know," he said shrugging his shoulders broadly. "To stir up trouble, I reckon. I never once did look into a poet-book myself afeard that 'Paw' would take a switch to me. But the good reverend says the words are evil and deceitful. And I believe him."

"Then why would anyone want to read them?" the seven year-old asked her sixth question.

Joshua was patient. "Time was," he explained, "folks used to read them there poet-books 'stead of doing their chores. The words were smooth and easy. Made 'em forget what they s'pposed to be doin'. They would dream 'bout the night when it was day, pretend to be others when they weren't, and travel to fancy worlds that can't never be. When folks finally woke up from their daydreams, they realized they had nothin' at all. Most of 'em became unhappy, and begun to make war on others to git what they ain't got—"

An ancient farmer, wearing worn-out overalls, a grimy red bandana, and a greasy straw hat, interrupted the boy's explanation. "Poetry intoxicates the brain, filling folks with uncontrollable desires. That there is a scientific fact."

"Have you ever read any 'po-et-tree'?" Martha looked up at him, her bright eyes twinkling as she repeated the new word to herself.

The farmer's corpse-like features squeezed themselves out of shape. "Young lady, that's again't the law," he replied after a moment's hesitation. "Why just last month, the good folks in Green township done tarred-and-feathered a school teacher for simply collecting them there poet-books."

"I hear told they's fixin' to start hangin' them fellas as well," another old-timer interjected. "They done got rid of all the scientists and politicians already. They's been hangin' poets and philosophers for the better part of a year. Don't rightly make sense why they's so fired up to start executin' teachers now when so many of them done run off like scared jackrabbits."

"Sure it do! Who'd you think filled them other fellas with so much hogwash? Teachers!" The ancient farmer placed both thumbs behind the bib of his overalls in a defensive posture. "Besides we have a civic duty to protect these children, and others like 'em, from the wrongdoers who done led us down this path to ruin. Can't never risk them bringin' down another firestorm upon us with their ed-ge-cation."

"Wendell, how'd you reckon they's goin' to do that with a handful of books?" his contemporary countered, trying to push the children aside.

"T'ain't the books, Griswald," he admonished the other man. "It's the ideas that are evil!"

Griswald shook his head. "I done heard the folks in the next township are usin' a lottery," he reported, thumping the other man's chest with the tips of his arthritic fingers.

"That don't make no sense at all!" Wendell exclaimed, thumping him back with the full force of the fingers of both hands. "We don't need no damn fool lottery to tell us what we's already knows."

Martha tugged like a gentle breeze on the leg of the ancient farmer's overalls. "How do you know somethin's bad if you never—"

But Joshua did not wait for her to finish. "Sis, we got to hurry if we want to git a good spot for the hangin'," he lied, pulling her hand away and dragging her to the other side of the square.

The little girl could not understand his haste.

*   *   *   *   *

For an hour and a half, the two children stomped their feet and rubbed their arms up-and-down to keep warm. Once the cold, morning rain had given way to a damp, afternoon chill, a murmur of impatience moved uneasily through the crowd.

"How much longer we got to wait, Josh?" Martha asked, blowing into her stone-white, cupped hands.

"Just a few more minutes," her brother replied. "The good Reverend likes to give condemned men every opportunity to repent before they's hung. I reckon there's nothin' more Christian a man could do."

Martha nodded and stared ahead, beyond the ruins of some ancient structure, to the place on the hill where Reverend Underwood preached his weekly sermons. She then scanned across the skeletons of other structures and watched two figures, one leading the other, emerge from the mist-shrouded rubble. Once they had approached the town square, she recognized the harsh, chiseled features of the parson but did not know what to make of the stranger. Martha felt her heart skip a beat and her mouth go suddenly dry as he filled her field of vision.

"For Christsakes, Reverend," decried the ancient farmer, "that man ought to have been hung by now!"

Reverend Underwood turned momentarily to melt the impatient man down in his tracks with a deadly glare, then exhaled a cold, icy breath. "Some of you fellows want to give me a hand?"

There was a slight hesitation before five men, one of them Martha's father, came forward to ready the prisoner for the gallows.

Three of them stood by with their farm tools braced as weapons, while two others tied the condemned man's hands behind his back, passed a heavy rope through his bindings, and lashed his arms tightly to his sides. Then, crowding very close to him with their arms always in a careful, caressing grasp, the five volunteers marched him quickly from the town square and up a narrow slope. The poet moved along quite unresisting, yielding his arms limply to their bonds and his legs to their faststep, as though he hardly noticed or cared what was happening.

Martha, Joshua, and the other members of the community followed closely behind at a safe distance.

Directly ahead, the gallows stood on a small hill which was overgrown with tall prickly weeds - the kind that grew on gravestones, forgotten highways, and anything that was dead. A solitary rope dangled from the central crossbar that was supported between two beams anchored to a wooden scaffold. The hangman, dressed in a soiled white robe and pointed hood, snapped the trap door shut with his lever, and stood back, waiting.

Martha Goodman could feel her heart beating faster with each forward step.

Though awkwardly trying to keep pace with her brother's long stride, the little girl finally stumbled and fell on the ragged edges of the broken pavement. Much to Martha's dismay, the other community members ignored her plight and hurried to form a rough circle around the gallows. Moments later, when they reached the hill, the two children had to push through the ring of adults to find a place in front. But as they struggled through the crowd, Reverend Underwood stepped forward and brought all movement to a halt with a singular action. He removed the death warrant from his black, ministerial robes.

"Thomas Worthington Meadows," he read the poet's name aloud, "you have been charged with sedition, treason, blasphemy, public reading and exhibition of forbidden literary works, and other acts which have contributed to the moral and spiritual decay of this township. Legally tried, according to the laws of this territory, you were found guilty of all charges and sentenced to be hanged by the neck until dead. Do you have any final words before sentence is carried out?" Reverend Underwood gave him several moments to answer, but when the poet failed to respond, the reverend simply added, "May God have mercy on your everlasting soul."

With that, and a subtle nod from the town elders, two of the volunteers, gripping the condemned man more closely than before, half held half pushed him to the gallows and helped him clumsily mount the stairs to the scaffolding. Once he reached the main platform, twenty feet above, the faceless hangman took charge. He led the poet to a fixed position over the trap door and fitted the dangling rope around his neck.

For a long time there was only the sound of the bitter. October wind blowing through the shattered ruins. Then, as the noose was finally tightened, the condemned man broke his silence:

> "Awake, O north wind; and come,
> thou south; blow upon my garden,
> that the spice there may flow out . . ."

Martha listened closely to the poet's words; they were not urgent like a prayer of salvation or fearful like a cry for help but soft, sweet, and lyrical. A kind of music to her ears.

> "Let my beloved come into this
> garden and eat of its pleasant fruits . . ."

Apparently deaf to his words though standing next to him on the gallows, the anonymous hangman produced a small burlap bag, like a flour sack, and pulled it roughly down over the condemned man's face. But the words, muffled only slightly by the cloth, still persisted:

> "Until daybreak, and the shadows
> flee away, I will sleep amidst the
> fountain of the garden and in the
> well of the living waters and by the
>
> rivers of Babylon . . ."

While she watched the hangman step back and stand ready at his lever, Martha Goodman felt uneasy. She could hear nothing evil or sacrilegious in the poet's words, and wondered why they all feared him so much. Around her, some of the community members were licking chapped lips; others eagerly sucked in the cold, damp air and let it hiss out between clenched teeth; still others anxiously counted down the seconds. One woman, with tears in her eyes, repeated, over and over, "Oh, kill him quickly! Get it over with! Stop that infernal noise!"

Only Martha stood apart, silent in her appreciation for his verse. Knowing in her heart she could no longer remain with them, she stepped out of the ring and walked toward the gallows.

Suddenly Reverend Underwood burst forward, shoving the little girl aside and shouting "Enough!" He then turned to the hangman and made a swift, fierce motion with his right hand. The hooded hangman responded to his command by pulling down on the lever. There was a loud, clanking noise, then dead silence as the condemned man plunged thirteen feet through the trap door.

Martha instantly closed her eyes, praying the rope would break. But when she heard a loud snap, she opened them to find the poet dangling with his toes pointed straight down, slowly revolving, as dead as the ruined town that lay around them.

She shrieked and started to cry. Her wailing was the only sound that could be heard for miles.

*　　*　　*　　*　　*

At five o'clock the Goodman family was escorted to their horse-and-buggy by Reverend Underwood, who lifted the seven year-old girl into the buckboard with her brother. While the adults conversed for a few moments in the chilly night air, Martha turned to look at the solitary figure on the hill.

"Will he just hang there all night?" she whispered to Joshua.

He turned and touched her shoulder. "I reckon, and probably hang there a spell tomorrow--so's people can recollect what his world nearly done to ours."

"But his words were so beautiful—"

"Hush your mouth, girl!" he exclaimed, clamping a hand over her mouth with cool authority. "Do you want 'Paw' and the reverend to hear you? There be a lot things you're too young to understand now, but when you git older everythin' will become crystal clear."

The little girl pulled away from his grasp and sat back around, silently, not speaking, listening to the adults exchange their fond farewells. Then, as the carriage began to move down the dark October road for home, Martha Goodman recited the poet's words secretly to herself, committing them to memory.

She understood all too well.

Night of Passage

Though its origins may have been lost in the cave etchings of primeval mythology, obscured by the superstitions of folklore, exploited by the "penny-dreadfuls" of Victorian melodrama, or trivialized by television shows and motion pictures, the vampire has remained a popular subject for thousands of years. Part of its popularity has to do with the wealth of metaphors vampires have represented, from reckless youth to eternal life or from sexual seduction to sexual domination. Like many authors, I have been fascinated with vampires as both characters and metaphors for years. But I'm not as interested in the throat-ripping exploits or the existential angst of vampires as I am with their origins and their interaction with humans. In "Night of Passage," I examine their mating rituals.

Jack Mitchell could no longer sleep; in fact, he didn't think he'd ever sleep again.

He opened his eyes in the darkness, for he again sensed movement near him, but he did not move. Only his eyes searched the darkness, and in the pale light of dawn which crept through the patio drapes he saw that everyone was still asleep. When he heard the crash of morning waves upon the beach, Mitchell let out a deep sigh, realizing that he had only imagined the movement, like a thousand other times that night.

The young college Sophomore raised his head to the light and tried to shake away the nightmare, but the images were still as crimson clear as the blood on his pillow. Flashing neon lights. Crowded boardwalk. Shapely blonde co-ed. Teeth ripping flesh.

He got out of bed and made certain the drapes were drawn tightly shut. Then, pulling his pillow apart, he stuffed the bloodied, cotton slip between the mattresses. The room hadn't been cleaned in almost a week, so he wasn't concerned that the maid would find his little secret. And even if she did, she'd probably think it was a valued trophy, proof that one of the guys in the room had wacked a virgin.

Jack Mitchell paused for a long, silent moment, then hurried over the lifeless bodies in the room on his way to the head. He thought that he was going to be sick again, but the nausea soon passed. Awkwardly, he reached up and flushed the toilet; but the fixture gurgled and sloshed, mocking him. He had forgotten it didn't work. Nothing worked in the cheap, flea-bitten motel room, except the television, and that was stuck on one channel.

Returning from the bathroom, he turned the set on and adjusted the volume so it would not disturb his sleeping companions. Jack then curled into a prenatal position on the edge of the bed with the hope of losing himself in the noiseless static. He wanted to believe that this was all part of a bad dream and that he would be waking soon; but the images kept coming back to haunt him, replacing those that appeared on the screen. Flashing neon lights. Crowded boardwalk. Shapely blonde co-ed. Teeth ripping—

"—flesh. Details are sketchy at this hour, but it appears that the badly-decomposed body of a twenty-two year-old, white female was discovered about an hour before dawn in an alley way adjacent the Buccaneer motel. The apparent cause of death was shock, induced by massive blood loss—" an unfamiliar voice resounded in the back of his head with a gravelly tone.

Mitchell shook himself awake. For about half a moment, he wasn't certain if the television images were real or part of his nightmare; but, as his ears strained for sound and he caught the news bulletin in mid-sentence, he became painfully aware of reality. And panic began to rise.

"Since there was no evidence of a struggle, sexual assault, or robbery, police detectives believe the young woman probably knew her assailant; but they are not ruling out the possibility that the crime may be drug-related. Although the victim's name and address are being withheld pending notification of the next of kin, Eyewitness News reporter Lisa McLellan will bring us a statement from the medical examiner, explaining the body's advanced state of decomposure, later this afternoon during our five o'clock broadcast," the newscaster continued. "County officials do stress extreme caution for anyone going out tonight to watch the lunar eclipse—"

Omigod, he mouthed with no wind behind it.

Jack stared at the television screen for several moments, his eyes trying to focus in disbelief. It wasn't a nightmare, or some bad dream. She was dead, and he alone knew who was responsible. He had torn a great hole in her neck and, like some wild beast of the jungle, had drunk her blood. That thought sent shudders of fear and revulsion racing up and down his body.

"Hey, would you mind turning that shit off!" a familiar voice shouted angrily from the sea of lifeless bodies.

Mitchell was silent for another moment, then ran to the bathroom to throw up.

Fifteen minutes later, Jack staggered back into the room, holding his stomach, a small dribble of blood at the corner of his mouth. Awkwardly, he reached for the volume control, then noticed that the television set was cold. Either someone in the room had already turned it off or he was having one helluva nightmare! The young man rubbed the sleep from his eyes, then touched himself all over. Had he just awoken from a bad dream, or was it still going on? He shook his head in confusion and looked around the room. When his eyes reached the slight indentation in the mattress, he knew that it was all too real.

Pulling on a pair of cut-off jeans, a T-shirt, and a pair of Reeboks, he decided to go out to the beach. Down there, on the Strip, there'd be people, thousands of revelers like himself, and maybe he'd be able to forget the images of her death. Jack gathered up the bloodied pillow case, hid it in his beach towel, and stopped by the motel dumpster on his way to the beach.

Outside the motel room, the blast of warm, tropical air instantly reminded him where he was and what he was supposed to be doing there. Winter in the Northeast had been incredibly bitter that year, and he'd come to Daytona Beach, like a thousand other college students, for the annual rite of passage, known as Spring Break. In fact, he and his best friend Mike had driven over twenty-one hours straight to reach Florida, and all he had wanted to do was relax and catch some rays. But the guys, with whom they had arranged to share a room, had other plans. Every night, they partied until dawn, drank several cases of beer, and tried to fuck every willing co-ed that they could. His holiday turned into one long blur of drunken misadventures and days spent on the beach, trying to sleep off his hangover. That is, until that warm night he met her . . .

Jack recalled the night Suzanne wandered into one of his friend's noctural orgies in technicolor detail. She was reserved, elegant, the most perfect woman that he had ever met, and not at all the type of airhead who attended college parties. He remembered how uncomfortable she seemed at the party, and how she responded to his suggestion that they take a long walk on the beach. They walked, for what seemed like hours, talking about the many different things that they had in common. They then sat by the water's edge and tried to count the stars in heaven before the dawn whisked them away. She was everything that he wanted in a woman, and Jack arranged to spend each successive night with her. When they were apart, he noticed a strange, empty sensation in his stomach that felt like love.

Thinking about Suzanne brought a momentary smile to his face, but that was quickly erased by the images that were so firmly implanted in his brain. He struggled for a moment with those thoughts, then tried to concentrate on the beauty around him.

The beach was a golden yellow, but at the water's edge a rubble of shell and algae took its place. Fiddler crabs bubbled and sputtered in their holes in the sand, as young people chased frisbees along the shore. Tropical winds raced over the waves and turned the blue water white, while overhead the hot, Florida sun maintained its silent, patient vigil.

In the heat of the day Jack Mitchell sat down by the water's edge and relaxed. He needed some time to think, to put the events of the last twelve hours into perspective, then, maybe, he'd know what to do. Covering his head with a beach towel to keep the sun off, he laid back and closed his eyes. The ceaseless dull hum of the beating waves was very comforting, and he eventually drifted off into a deep sleep.

At about four o'clock in the afternoon, Jack stirred from another nightmare. He dreamt that he was being buried alive, and he felt like he was suffocating. Scarcely able to breathe, he clawed at the beach towel, his hands moving in symbolic struggle. He then cried out in a guttoral voice and sat up suddenly, his eyes wide and his nostrils flaring. But it was nothing more than a bad dream, and as he glanced around at the people on the beach, he realized just how foolish his actions must have appeared.

Thoroughly shit-faced with embarassment, he gathered up his beach towel and headed for the Strip.

Mitchell bought some french fries at a sidewalk counter and smothered them with the traditional condiments, but he couldn't eat them. Their golden yellow coloring reminded him of her blonde hair, and the redness of the Heinz ketchup reminded him of the blood on his pillow. He threw them in a trash can and walked further down the street. In fact, he wandered the boardwalk for several hours trying to loose himself in the sights and sounds; but every place Jack went he was reminded of her.

When the sun went down, his thoughts of her became cold in the night air. The temperature was actually quite warm, but he felt chilled and decided to return to the motel for a windbreaker.

"Hey, yo—"

Jack heard a familiar voice call him, and he went over to the sidewalk bar where his best friend was relaxing. "Mike, am I glad to see you," he said, slipping into a lounge chair next to him. "I think I'm in some deep shit, and you gotta help me!"

"You look really wasted, man," his friend replied. "Why don't you chill out, and have a brew?"

"Remember that girl I was with—"

"Oh, her," Mike scowled, taking a sip from his beer and slapping the bottle down hard on the table. "Yeh, I remember her. Who wouldn't remember a woman who looks like she just stepped right out of the *Sports Illustrated Swimsuit Issue*? But I've seen her type before, in a hundred different places, and I know how women like that operate on guys like you—"

Jack Mitchell looked at his best friend in surprise.

"—I mean, look at you," he continued, his voice flat and blunt. "She's turned you into some kind of zombie. In fact, ever since you started hanging out with her, you've changed into a totally different person! You sleep all day, then stay out all night." He took another swig of his drink and added, "I'm supposed to be your best buddy, and yet, the last three days, you haven't had a moment for me. Like you wrote me off, or something—"

"Mike, please," Jack pleaded, his friend's words hitting home. "I'm sorry. You're right. But I really do need your help."

"Okay, okay, okay," he replied, nodding his head in union with a drink. "Did you and what's-her-name have a fight?"

"Not what's-her-name. Su—zanne," Jack whispered in response, the two syllables of her name falling heavily upon his breath. "And it was more than just a fight. I think I may have killed her—"

Mike broke out laughing. "Oooooo, Mitchell, you're sooo cool," he said. "You don't have to boast about your conquests. Those love bites on your neck tell me what a real ladykiller you are."

Jack reached over and grabbed Mike by the lapels of his denim jacket, surprising his friend almost as much as himself. *I'm not joking,* " he protested. "I *really did kill Suzanne.*"

His friend's eyes bulged slightly in their sockets, stunned by the unexpected fury. He took a deep breath, then peeled Jack's fingers from his lapels. "You've turned into a real nut case, Mitchell," he growled. "The two of you were made for each other."

Jack eased back in his chair. "I'm sorry. I don't know what got into me—"

"Sure! Why don't you just get the fuck out of here," Mike exclaimed, before taking a long drink from his beer.

Mitchell rose to his feet sluggishly, looking dazed, as though he had lost his only friend in the whole world. He walked forward a few steps, his eyes travelling up and down the Strip yet apparently not seeing anything. He paused, then turned back around slowly. For a moment or two he said nothing. Finally, with a weary sigh, he said softly, "I was telling you the truth."

"That joke is really wearing thin," Mike said flatly. "Considering that she stopped by here a few moments ago, she looked pretty good for a fuckin' corpse. Now tell me something I don't know."

Jack's eyes snapped open. "What? Where is she? Which way did she go?"

"How the hell should I know? Look for her on the Strip—"

Mitchell raced off in search of Suzanne. He didn't know whether he should believe what his friend had said, yet he found himself yearning for it to be true. For several hours, he looked in bars, restaurants, and motel lobbies. He looked down alley ways and in amusement arcades. But he could not find any trace of her.

Frustrated, he paused at the edge of the beach and watched the revelers as they celebrated the passage of the moon into the earth's shadow.

"Jack—" her voice called to him from a cabana hut on the beach.

The young college Sophomore shivered, though he knew it wasn't cold, and his bronze, Coppertone tan turned snow white as he followed her voice into the darkness. For a split second Suzanne's shape shimmered, like that of a ghost, and Jack wasn't certain that she was real. Then, as her amorphous shadow thickened and solidified, and she moved into the moonlight, he could see her quite clearly. Her cool, blonde hair fell softly on her shoulders, and her face and hands were pale against the vivid redness of her lips. She wore an exotic and elegant, black, twist-top bikini that was covered by a transparent red, oversized shirt, which flowed and billowed in the night air.

"I dreamt you were dead—"

"Since we've been apart, I've been neither alive nor dead," Suzanne replied, moving toward him. "You are that which gives me life." Her arms snaked around his shoulders, and she kissed him once long and hard on the lips, with a fierce tenderness that was almost without passion.

At first, Jack Mitchell stood rigid and uncertain, his mouth trembling under hers. He was afraid to move, afraid to react, afraid that she was some phantom who would disappear at his slightest touch. But, as she pressed her cool lips to his and wrapped her hands around his neck, Jack's fears were replaced by intense desire. Cautiously, he traced the outline of her body with his fingertips. Her beauty was so strange and overwhelming that he allowed himself a moment to bask in it, as if it were any natural phenomenon like sunshine or fragrant air. Then, satisfied that she was real and no ghostly apparition, he pulled Suzanne closer to him and kissed her deeply.

The two lovers kissed in the shadow of the cabana hut, gradually turning in each other's arms, while, above their heads, the earth's dark umbra reached in passionate embrace for the moon. Finally, after several long minutes, as darkness slowly crept over the beach, Jack's mouth slid away from hers. "Suzanne," he whispered softly in her right ear, "you are the most beautiful, exciting thing that has ever happened to me."

She didn't seem to be surprised. "Such flattery must come easily to a college man, like yourself, who has known so many young co-eds."

"Not one of them has ever touched me in the way that you do," he said, kissing her pale cheeks and running his hands through her silky, blonde hair. "When I look into your eyes, I feel—"

"What do you feel?" she asked coldly.

Jack drew Suzanne away from the shadows and into the light of the diminishing moon. "I feel a burning desire that only you can satisfy," he replied, staring into her eyes. "A thirst that only you can quench."

"Have you any idea how long I've waited for someone to say that to me?" she said, turning around carefully and stepping back into the cover of darkness. "But you must realize that I am not like the others. I do not simply give my love away freely, without expecting something in return."

Jack was startled by her statement. "Like what? My fraternity pin? A ring? Tell me what price you put on love, and I will get it for you."

Suzanne glanced at him, amused.

"I am fond of gifts, but not mere material things," she said, without enthusiasm, as if her attention had been momentarily diverted. "I think the greatest gift a man can give a woman is his innocence, but that he can only give once."

Jack Mitchell raised an eyebrow at the mysterious blonde and started to ask her what she meant. Then he thought better of it and remained silent. He knew exactly what she meant, but that was one gift he had already given away. Five years ago, to be precise, to Cathy Keaney on the hood of his brother's Camaro. He would have to tell her the truth.

Jack took a deep breath, then shrugged his shoulders. "I'm afraid I--"

"Oh, that is a pity, but I'm sure that someone who is as bright and imaginative as you are can think of something else to give me. Perhaps you need only—" She left the sentence unfinished and moved toward the water's edge, looking wistfully into the darkness.

Jack hesitated a moment to collect his thoughts, then turned to face her. "I'm not certain what you want from me—" As he said that, his gaze met ers, and he instantly knew what she wanted. He also sensed that she attached great importance to how he phrased it. "—but I offer you everything that I am. I offer you my life."

Suzanne smiled knowingly, "—forever."

Jack saw a shadow move across her face, and he turned his eyes toward the night sky.

"The lunar eclipse," she sighed and curled around him, resting her head on his shoulders. "The darkest moment across the entire planet! What a joy it would be if that moment lasted forever!"

"That's an odd thing to say."

"Are you aware that many nocturnal creatures mate for life during the lunar eclipse?"

"Oh, really? I didn't know that—" he replied, distracted by the celestial passage of the moon into the earth's dark shadow.

"Jack, there's something that I must tell you, but you must promise not to be afraid."

He grunted his acknowledgment, only partially aware of what she had said.

"I am a creature of the night—" Suzanne's voice deepened, and her breath became noticeably foul. "—and you are the life which gives me sustenance."

Jack Mitchell felt the tiny hairs raise on the back of his neck, and he turned around very slowly, in order to give the bad feeling plenty of time to go away. But it didn't. He had been so absorbed in the eclipse that he hadn't noticed Suzanne's metamorphosis. While he had been busy watching the night sky, she had exchanged her human form for something more beastly. In fact, his heart skipped a beat once he had completed the turn and saw what she had become.

Gone were the elegant and mysterious good looks that had attracted him to the blonde. The real Suzanne—if that was truly her name--was some ancient, misshapen creature that owed its development to no line of earthly evolution that he knew. It was dark and reptilian, with dry, withered skin, a long black snout, pointed, leathery ears, and bulging, lifeless eyes. Although the thing looked like some hideous cross between a panther, a snake, and a bat, it most closely resembled a gargoyle, one of those carved, mythical figures that he had seen on several old buildings in New York City. When the creature smiled at him, he trembled, and for the first time noticed its teeth. They were long and very, very sharp.

"What's wrong, Jack? Don't you want me anymore?"

Mitchell shrank back in horror. "What is this? Some sort of joke?" he breathed. "Where is Suzanne?"

"She is here, within me, as are all the others," it explained, as the hump-like mass between its shoulder blades effortlessly extended into webbed wings, flapped once, then retracted. "You see, we creatures of the night consume not only blood but also looks, personality—all the things that make one human."

"But I loved her—"

"Then you will love me."

Jack was filled with a sudden loathing that made him sick. "How could I possibly love the thing that killed her?" he shouted angrily. "You're an ugly, disgusting monster—"

The creature stretched one of its talons up to stop his lips. "No, no, Jack, you don't understand," it said thoughtfully. "I didn't kill anyone, particularly not Suzanne. I loved her very much, just as you did. She's a part of me now, the part that brought me to you. And soon, you'll be a part of her. Nothing in the world will ever come between the two of you again."

"Who. or rather, what are you?"

"I can be anything that you desire—" The creature replied, as it resumed its human appearance, changing into a variety of guises --both male and female--before returning to Suzanne.

"That's not an answer!" he protested. "What are you? Where do you come from?"

Suzanne opened her mouth and slid her swollen tongue across razor-sharp fangs. "You'll soon have answers to all your questions—"

"—once you steal my body from me."

"You're wrong, Jack," she said softly. "We never take that which is not given to us freely."

Mitchell was gravely silent. He wanted to run, but his legs felt like two hundred pound weights caught in cement. He wanted to scream, but his throat felt like it was tied with a hangman's knot. The best that he could manage was a quiet whimper which sounded more animal than human. This wasn't happening, he tried to tell himself, but his thoughts were less than convincing.

"Don't be afraid," she implored. "There's nothing to be afraid of. I mean, really, it's not so bad—"

Jack swallowed twice to find his voice. "But the blood on my pillow?"

"I'm sorry, Jack," she sighed, drawing near him. "The conversion process takes several days, and your wounds may not have healed properly—"

"Wounds?" he mumbled the word.

Jack Mitchell felt his lower neck, and suddenly became very weak, like he was going to faint. There were two puncture marks that he hadn't noticed before. His friend Mike had called them love bites, but they had little to do with love.

Suzanne approached him and placed her hands on Jack's face, the long forefingers probing at his temples. Her gaze never met Jack's. She seemed to look straight through him. He closed his eyes, hoping to erase the nightmare, but the woman's image remained, cold and expressionless. He tried to turn away, but she only grasped hold tighter, pulling him ever so firmly into her web like that of a black widow spider with its mate.

"I know what it's been like for you. Lots of lovers and no love," she whispered in his ear. "But after tonight, you'll never be lonely again. You'll be part of me, and I'll be part of you—"

Suzanne kissed his neck, rubbing her teeth along the cords of taut muscle. Then slowly, gently, she pierced the first layer of flesh, searching for the hot, red liquid that gave her life. She eventually reached the vein, and drank from it hungrily, consuming not only blood but Jack Mitchell's entire being.

Blood ran across his shoulders and down Jack's strong, muscular chest. His body shook in terror and ecstasy, then collapsed weakly into her arms. Jack could feel his lifeforce seeping away, but there was nothing that he could do. She retained such a tight hold over him. With all the remaining strength that he could muster, the young man tried to call for help; but his voice was lost in the sound of cheering revelers as they celebrated their peculiar rite of passage.

Resigned to his fate, Jack Mitchell turned his weary eyes to the night sky and watched the moon emerge from the other side of the earth's dark umbra. For an instant, he was back in his motel room, gliding off into blissful sleep; then, in the next, he was holding Suzanne in a passionate embrace. Finally, after several long minutes, Jack's mouth slid away from the neck, and he let the body slip from his arms, as it had a thousand times before, in a thousand different places.

The young college Sophomore stood up straight, turned toward the Strip, and smiled. Neon lights flashed. The beach was crowded, and thousands of young men and women were his for the taking. But first, the part of him that was Jack remembered some unfinished business with one of his roommates, and licked his lips in anticipation.

Mike was in for one helluva surprise.

Interfacing Rush

For three years, I ran a welfare office for the City of Baltimore, and watched as the gulf between the haves and the have-nots widened. My heart went out to each of those predominantly African-American women as they struggled to work themselves out of poverty in order to make a better life for their children. Some made it out of the projects and into a better lifestyle; most did not—most were crushed under the grinding wheels of politicians who paid them lip-service but little else. So, in writing "Interfacing Rush," I tried to imagine what it would be like to be the downtrodden. I knew that I wouldn't be able to write a convincing African American as a protagonist, without sounding condescending or simply naive, so I inverted the world and wrote this very dark parallel universe.

The first time I saw Joshua Rush, I thought he was either an undertaker or flesh peddler; only later did I learn the truth.

I had been hustling some rare hybrid opiates down on Canal Street, trying to score time on the farside for my matrix junkie friend, when Rush's vintage '93 Cadillac (with armor plating and conversion) peeled 'round the corner. It hovered, for a moment, above the curb, then deposited the four-hundred pound niggah and his elite goon squad on the pavement below. I didn't know who he was then, and normally wouldn't have paid him any mind. Lenny and me had seen more than our share of fat freebooters in Central City. But it was hard not to notice the effect this man had on the other gutter rats as he lumbered into view. Whores, fellow drug dealers and shills seemed to melt away into the blessed shadows with his approach. Homeless people, who had been gathered around trash can fires for warmth, now huddled in doorways, shivering in their tattered clothing. Packs of roving teens, once the scourge of that concrete jungle, scattered to the dark alleyways, taking their sidewalk terrorism and a handful of scared pedestrians with them. I could only think of two kinds of men who provoked that much fear, and knew better than to cross either of them.

As Joshua Rush and his goons worked their way down the street—stopping first to rough up several punked-out rockers too stupid or too stoned to get out of his way, then beating up a young whore who didn't know any better—Lenny slid down from his loft and slowly edged himself along the slippery pavement on hands and knees. "Time to go, Jack," he whispered.

"No, we haven't scored nearly enough juice," I replied, determined to hold my ground. I had faught much too hard to earn that place on Canal Street, and I wasn't going to give it up, even if it meant I took some heat. "Besides, I promised to meet someone here. Someone who might be able to help us out—"

"So, where is this guy?"

"I don't know. I'm not even sure what he looks like anymore. I haven't seen him in years."

"Where you know him from?"

"New Tokyo," I said, without thinking, annoyed by his childish preoccupation with questions.

"The 'wars?" Lenny cried out in horror. "Oh, Christ, not the 'wars!"

Shit! I knew better than to mention that city in front of him, but it just sort of slipped out. We had spent the last two years trying to forget that city, trying to forget the CyberWars ever happened; but whenever I was being careless or callous, my disregard would send him right over the edge. Lenny had lost a lot during the 'wars. More than me. More than most people. One day, he had been a decorated cyberjock, one of those crazy systems' operators who plugged directly into the matrix, and the next, a disabled veteran— a computer junkie no longer capable of braving farside without the juice. He pretended that it didn't matter, but I knew better. I knew there were parts of him still back there, fighting those corporate battles, searching for **her**.

"—and it's starting all over again, just the way it did two years ago."

"Don't you start," I cut him off. "I warned you not to take that damned assigment in the first place. Why the hell didn't you listen to me?"

He turned and looked away. "Jack, she needed me—and I couldn't just let her go alone."

"Yeah, well, look where it got you."

"What if they catch up to us again, Jack? What if they put us in separate cells?" his voice raised in panic. "I don't think I can stand that torture again, not those endless hours of pain—"

I gathered him into my arms and stroked his hair with gentle caresses of reassurance. "Don't worry, pal. I'll take care of you. Nothin's gonna happen."

Lenny shook his head. His eyes narrowed and his mouth widened in terror as the shadows of Joshua Rush and his goons closed in. I sensed them too, and placed my friend back down on the pavement. But the instant after I turned around, that fat sonuvabitch was in my face, regarding me with dark, lifeless eyes. He then smiled, his mouth a lost graveyard, the pearly white teeth standing like forgotten tombstones in the blackness. Rush never said a word to either of us; but as he swaggered past my friend, he began to bellow with a pointless laughter which he carried for several blocks.

Lenny awkwardly seized my lower limbs and held on tightly like a frightened infant to its mother. He wanted instant comfort and reassurance, but I had no more to give him. I was just as confused and frightened as he was; in fact, any other person would have known that by the loud beating of my heart, but not Lenny. He just held onto me with his fearful embrace, totally oblivious to everything and everyone.

Within minutes of Rush's departure, Canal Street was once again teeming with familiar activity. Shills barked out commands from their familiar spots, coercing passersby into live sex shows. Cheap-smelling whores walked their familiar beats, offering bargain rates to those who could least afford a little intimacy. Drug dealers sold their familiar poisons to junkies with that greedy, vacant look. Homeless people moved back to their familiar fires for warmth, while handfuls of teenagers emerged from barren alleyways to form their familiar packs. In the distance, even the shiny, high-tech towers of the city had a familiar purpose reminding us that Joshua Rush and other freebooters like him were still in charge.

I'd had enough of those gutter rats for one day, and suddenly that included Lenny, too. He must have seen something of this in my expression, for he abruptly released me and hobbled up the porch steps to his loft. I sat down for a few minutes with my head in my hands, already regretting I had made plans to meet anyone and wishing I was miles away. Then I stood up and wandered down to the curb.

I hadn't taken more than two steps when I first heard the whispers of my name from a familiar voice, and turned toward the shadows. Marc Kantner, pale as death, with his hands plunged like weights in the pockets of his trousers, was standing in the darkness of the abandoned monorail platform, glaring tragically into my eyes, repeatedly whispering my name.

"Marc, is that you?" I asked, attempting to penetrate the dark void between us.

With his hands still in his pockets, Kantner descended several steps, pushed through the rusted turnstyle, and drifted towards me, into the light. As he crossed the street, he paused momentarily to glance up and down the block with a strange, puzzled look in his face. He was still the tall, cadaverous man that I remembered, but the ruby-red lips, long luscious eyelashes and powdered milky white complexion bespoke a feminine side I had never known. When he moved closer to me, I noticed that his eyebrows had been plucked and then drawn on again at an acute angle to match his other razor-sharp features. His androgenous appearance was somewhat of a shock to me, but I tried not to show my disapproval.

"I'm awfully glad to see you again."

He considered my words for a moment, then nodded his head without expression.

"You know," I added, feeling somewhat guilty, "I always meant to stay in touch."

"Forget it, Taylor," he protested with a weary sigh, the words no louder than a whisper. "We all promised a lot of things that we really didn't mean. Why should you have been any different from the rest?"

His voice was so solemn, as if the memory of those days still haunted him in the way they haunted Lenny. For a moment I suspected that he was pulling my leg, but a glance at him convinced me otherwise. There was nothing I could say in my defense, for Kantner was absolutely right. But it still pissed me off to admit the promises we had made to each other under fire were just as hollow as the ones we never kept in the real world. Perhaps that was all the more reason why I had to keep the one promise I had made to Lenny.

"So, what's wrong with your buddy there?" Marc asked, more out of politeness than genuine interest.

"Those assholes at the Sci Tech Corporation grabbed him during a mission, tortured him, then pumped his body full of a synthetic form of amyotrophic lateral sclerosis," I replied. "The really fucked up part is that the disease doesn't outright kill you. It just slowly eats away your nervous system until you're nothing but a fuckin' vegetable."

"Poor bastard—"

"All those years we were supporting Jerry's kids, they were developing it as a goddamn weapon."

"—why haven't you taken him to the Euthanasia Office for disposal?"

Without thinking, I seized Marc by the lapels of his leather jacket and shoved him up against the wooden planks of an abandoned storefront. "He's a goddamn person, not some piece of trash!"

Kantner's pale blue eyes bulged strangely in their sockets, stunned by my sudden fury. He swallowed a deep breath, then pried my fingers from his lapels. "Christ, I didn't mean nothin' by it," he growled.

"I know you didn't, Marc. I'm just so fuckin' tired of always having to—"

He raised his hand to stop my words, looked at me with unforgettable reproach, then pulled a mysterious envelope from his jacket. "Look, here's the deal," Kantner explained coolly, placing the envelope into my hands. "Niggah I owe a couple of favors to in Central City asked me to line up an unlicensed cyberjock to interface with some half-assed program of his in cyberspace. He's offering ten grand, no questions asked, and I'll let you have it all if you and your friend there help me out."

I ripped open the envelope and thumbed through the greenbacks with disdain. "You want us to do business with some freebooter uptown."

"That's ten grand there," he insisted. "What difference does it make who calls the shots?"

"It makes a difference to me," I said defiantly, then turned to glean Lenny's endorsement. But my friend just sat there quietly in his loft with a confused look on his face that concealed a dozen questions or more. "When the 'wars were over, and people like Lenny were trying to put their lives back together, those cutthroats preyed upon ailing cities like the carpetbaggers who stole the old, Confederate South. They bought up businesses that had gone belly up during the great panic with their low-interest minority loans, and took over massive housing projects the government could no longer afford. What they couldn't control or influence, they hired street punks to burn. Eventually, they had enough juice to start controlling the information highways, and began raiding the corporations for their technology—"

"Spare me the fuckin' history lesson!" he barked with such suddenness that I started—it was the first time he had raised his voice above a whisper. Evidently it surprised him as much as it did me, for he bit down hard on his rosy-red lips and then, with a series of well practiced movements, took out a cigarette and began smoking.

"You don't have to remind me what kind of men we're dealing with here," he whispered between nervous puffs of smoke. "I know he's a raider, a piratech; but I'm also smart enough to know we're powerless to do anything without men like him."

"So, what's your cut in all of this?" I demanded.

Kantner took a long drag on his cigarette, then released the captured smoke slowly. "Does it really matter?"

"Yeah, it matters. I'd like to think my life is worth more than thirty pieces of silver."

He rejected my biblical allusion by raising his eyebrow in

disdain, but kept right on smoking. "He tore up a handful of markers I owed him. Wiped the slate clean," Marc said at last, throwing his cigarette to the pavement and snuffing the glowing cinder out with the toe of his shoe. "He also fixed it with the doctors so I could get the change."

"You frickin' bastard, you've already told him we'd do it."

Kantner stared at me without a word, and I knew in an instant I had guessed right. That look of betrayal in his eyes told me that whatever friendly intentions, whatever notions of goodwill he may have had, were definitely gone. I started to turn away, but he took a step after me and grabbed my arm.

"I didn't have much choice," he replied, "and now you don't either. He knows what the two of you look like. He knows your hangouts, your dealings, your contacts—everything about your lives. And he won't leave you alone until you've completed the job—"

"You speak about him as if he were god."

"He is god—the only god." Marc looked at the shiny steel buildings in the distance with rapture. "He is power—the only real power on earth."

"You've changed."

"Yeah, maybe I have. Maybe I've finally taken a good close look at the world, and grown up."

"But change isn't always a good thing," I said. "The man I knew years ago wouldn't have sold out his principles or his friends for a half dozen markers and some goddamned sex change."

"Change is a fact of life," he said, the well-rehearsed reply swelling over his tongue. "Resistance to change, to new ideas, is stupid. No, it's worse than stupid—it's futile, for it can end in only one way for you and your pal—death."

I plucked several one hundred dollar bills from the envelope and threw them in his face. "That's for the fuckin' lesson in psychology," I quipped. "Now why don't you get the hell out of here!"

Marc Kantner knelt down on the pavement and gathered up the greenbacks, stuffing them into the folds of his leather jacket. He then handed me a sliver of paper which, when examined under a nearby streetlight, revealed the name and address of our new employer. I turned back to confirm the time, but Kantner was no longer there. He had already disappeared into the shadows of the night. Only later did I learn, from a couple of the gutter rats I least despised, that Kantner had sold us out to the very same man we had encountered earlier that evening. I cursed the day I'd ever laid eyes on that androgenous asshole. .

*   *   *.   *   *

A few minutes before the nightly curfew, I gathered Lenny into my arms and started down the familiar path to home. We had not spoken all evening about what had transpired between Kantner and me, despite my friend's overwhelming curiosity. I just didn't know how to tell him that we were suddenly ten thousand dollars richer or that we had been betrayed by my former friend without evoking dozens of questions I was far too tired to answer. I decided to wait until after we had reached home, and he was comfortably tucked away in bed.

When my friend and me approached the abandoned building we called home, we were greeted by a flickering orange glow climbing on the side wall that formed strange dancing shadows. But it was the smell of food being cooked over a open fire that reached us first. Neither one of us had eaten much all day, and the thought of a well-grilled steak filled my stomach with a familiar grumbling sensation. I moved cautiously around the building, with Lenny still in my arms, and stepped into the open entryway. Several men, stripped to the waist of their greasy clothes, were seated crosslegged around the small fire. They were roasting a straggly dog on an old tire iron, and basting its carcass with a steak sauce they had made out of mud. Most residents of Canal Street never tasted fresh meat. They lived out of garbage cans, if they were lucky, while others hunted dogs, cats, rodents and people too sick or feeble-minded to get out of the way. One man with waist-length hair that was gathered into a ponytail rose slowly to his feet and beckoned us to dinner. Their crude weapons lay close at hand, long spears with arrowheads forged from sardine cans that glinted in the firelight.

Fearing that they might find either one of us more appetizing than the dog, I declined their invitation and broke for the shadows. Several blocks away, I had to stop running and put Lenny down in order to catch my breath, but I didn't sense we were in any danger. The squatters must have figured that we weren't worth the trouble, and decided to settle down to their greasy meal. If they had known I was carrying an envelope full of greenbacks, they would have hunted us down and killed us, then roasted our bodies over the open fire.

For a moment, I permitted that horrible thought to consume me, while I waited for the life to creep back into my arms and legs. Then I glanced at my friend, who was staring down the street in terror. He was again fighting that imaginary war, and we were in the trenches, climbing over fallen comrades.

I hoisted Lenny back into my arms, and started down one of the alleys. We soon passed the carcass of animal that had been half eaten, then left in the ashes of a smoldering fire, and I was instantly on guard. But the remnants of other ancient campfires, piles of human and animal bones, and scattered ashes convinced me that we had just stumbled upon some lost picnic ground where the hollow men come to feed. Our unexpected appearance must have frightened one of them away from his meal. At the end of the alley, a hunched figure, dressed in rags like a scarecrow, emerged from behind a fence, then scurried away, perhaps fearing that we were hunters. He disappeared so fast there was no time to ask him.

We followed the low whitewashed railroad fence for about a block and a half, then crossed under one of the viaducts to the other side, searching for a place to rest. The only building which still had part of its roof intact was a small brownstone sitting on the edge of a wasteland of twisted steel girders, wooden shards and concrete rubble. We slipped across the street without notice, then climbed the cracked, broken steps of that dead building and squatted down in its foreboding shadows to listen for signs of life.

Satisfied that we were alone, I carried Lenny to the second floor, and began looking around for ways to make our stay more comfortable. Towards the back of the building, I discovered several stained mattresses that whores had been using to entertain clients. It was a relatively simple matter to strip off the mattress covers and clean them up for one night's use. I also found some moth-eaten pillows and pieces of tattered linen that we could use as blankets. In the basement, I scrounged whatever food I could find from several traps the former owners had once used to catch rodents; it was obviously stale but still eatable. I tried to provide my friend with all the comforts of home, for I knew what I had to tell him would not be very pleasant.

After I had finished explaining what had happened, I pulled out the envelope and showed him the ten thousand dollars' worth of greenbacks. "We've got enough here," I continued in a soft whisper, "to make a fresh start some place else."

"You mean, run away—" Lenny raised his bushy gray eyebrows in polite inquiry.

"Hell, yes!"

"But what about Rush and his goons?"

"Fuck 'em. By the time they figure out we've doublecrossed them, we'll be long gone."

"Just how far do you think you'd get with a cripple?"

I shrugged, far too tired to answer. Finally, after a moment of awkward silence, I reached for my friend's hand and placed the envelope of money in his palm. "This is our chance to get out of here," I said, at last, "to finally blow this town."

"But we can't just leave her behind," he replied, raising the spectre of his lost love before my eyes and dressing it with flesh and bones.

"Rachel died over two years ago on the same mission that cost you your—"

"No, you're wrong, Jack." He looked around himself wildly, as if she were lurking in the shadows of this building, just out of his reach. "She is still alive. She's just trapped in cyberspace. But once I get to her, we're going to build a brand new life together," he said with a nod of determination.

"You fool, she's dead"—I repeated—"dead."

"No, you'll see," he persisted. "I'm going to beat that computer system and then fix everything just the way it was before, just the way she likes it—"

"Interfacing Rush could be very dangerous," I spoke through

gritted teeth, trying to ignore his last statement, but the painful look in his face wouldn't let me. "Do you know what 'dangerous' means?"

Lenny shook his head broadly.

"You could get hurt—"

"What more can they do to me," he sighed, fumbling for the right words, "that they haven't done already?"

At times, my friend was very hard to reason with. His simple, childlike logic was flawless, as if there was some great genius inside struggling to climb out of a worthless body. And yet when he would say things like that to me, I found myself hard-pressed to respond with anything as profound, so I just stuck to the facts. "Lenny," I reminded him, "your nervous system is so badly damaged now that any unnecessary shocks or strains could prove fatal." I knew he wasn't getting it, and rephrased my words in a way that would make him understand. "If there are any glitches or hidden sub-commands in his program, you could get fried."

"But I'll have the juice—"

"There's not enough juice in the entire world to protect you if something goes wrong during an illegal interface. You know that."

Lenny stared at me dumbly. "But I've gone to farside dozens of times since the 'wars."

"Can't you understand!" I cried in anger, knowing he really didn't understand. "The state-run program is far less risky than what you'd be facing for Rush. They've got safeguards built in, so that people don't get hurt. Their program is designed for recreation, not corporate warfare. You don't have to do this! We've got plenty of money now to buy our own computer time."

"But, Jack, don't you see," he replied, falling back on his inescapable logic. "The reason why I've never found her is that she must be trapped there, in some part of cyberspace that's restricted—"

"Sure . . . sure," I said with a wave of my hand. "But you'll never be able to help her if you get killed during the interface."

"I've got to try, Jack. I just can't run away and let her—" Lenny suddenly broke off and grasped his chest with a look of disbelief. His body grew rigid, and his breathing became heavy and uneven.

"What's the matter?" I asked, leaning forward and taking him into my arms.

"A pain in my chest."

"Since when have you been having chest pains?"

"About a month," he gasped. "I didn't want you to be worried so I never said nothin'."

"We've got to get you to a doctor."

Lenny sensed the concern in my voice. "You really think it's that bad?"

"No, it's probably nothing," I lied, "but we shouldn't take any chances."

"The truth."

I shook my head, and sighed. "The truth is I don't know. This disease affects people in different ways. Some live for twenty years or more, while others last less than a couple of months. The pain in your chest is a lot like the seizures you keep having—just one more sign that your body is starting to fail you."

"I don't really mind dying, you know," he revealed with a sigh of regret, "but I would just like one last crack at the matrix before I go."

"What's this bullshit about dying! We're going to get you patched up, good as new."

"Sure, like those doctors really care about what happens to a couple of derelicts like us," he said, seemingly gathering his wits together for one last, great burst of reason which never came. "Besides, we'd never get through their armed sentries."

I snatched the envelope from his gnarled fingers and held it in the air, about eye level. "We'll buy our way in if we have to."

"No," he protested weakly. For a moment I thought he was going to suggest that I take the money and run, but rather he continued prattling on about Rachel and his dream for their future. The money was now part of that dream, and he seemed reluctant to discuss any alternatives for its use. So I just listened for what may have been the second or thirty-second time, waiting for the pain in his chest to finally subside.

Lenny talked about her for several hours, and when his voice weakened, I think he rather half-expected me to pick up where he left off. Instead, I placed his head down gently on one of the pillows and pulled the tattered linen up over his shoulders. I then sat back against the open door and watched him drift off to that safe world beyond the darkness, which I did not have the courage to go myself. He believed in his dream—the promise that he could recover some lost part of himself that had gone into loving her. The dream was such a simple one, and must have seemed so close that he could hardly fail to grasp it each time he traveled to the farside. He did not know that it was already behind him, and all that waited ahead, for all of us, was pain and death.

*   *   *   *   *

I couldn't sleep all night; some ancient hunter-killer kept circling the neighborhood in search of illegal aliens and other expatriots, and I tossed half-sick between grotesque reality and savage, frightening nightmares. Towards dawn, I heard the sirens of a fire engine hurrying by on its way to burn someone's private library, and immediately I jumped out of bed and began to dress. I felt that I had something more to say to my friend, something to warn him about, and morning would be too late. But as I approached his room I realized that we had said everything the night before and there was really nothing left to talk about. I simply returned to the open doorway and sat down quietly in the shadows.

When he finally got up, Lenny leaned into the howling beast of wind, which blew through his broken window, and smiled. I sensed that he had gotten a good night's rest, and had not been bothered by the demons of war like so many sleepless nights before. I fed him the remains of our dinner, combed his hair and carried him into our makeshift bathroom. Once my friend had relieved himself, I helped him put on a pair of pants and a shirt I had stolen from a laundry line, and tied his shoes. The routine had been the same for nearly two years, and I prided myself on being able to knock it out in thirty minutes. But that day was different. That day, I felt like I was dressing him for the last time, and I was being purposely slow in an effort to memorize every last detail.

I hailed one of the gypsy cab drivers, brave enough to travel our streets, and paused to listen with Lenny as the armored vehicle screeched to a hault mere footsteps from the front door. I then hurried him into the backseat of the cab, and barked out a series of directions to the driver.

About half way between our home just off Canal Street and the steel towers of Central City, we passed through a desolate part of town that ran parallel to the railroad tracks for three miles. Bounded on one side by a small foul river that discharged all manner of medical and toxic waste into the lake, the small community was a metropolis of death and dying. Most of the buildings lay in ruin, with abandoned storefronts, burned-out shells and rat-infested housing projects forming the balance of the urban landscape. Junked cars filled the street, and pockets of light-trailing wispy gray smoke rose from the crumbling decay. And the sounds—not the sounds that most people associated with cities but the frenzied rhythms of jungle drums, automatic weapons and banshee screams—were so loud that you had to travel through the community with all the windows rolled up.

I had been born and raised in that small community, back in the days when most people left their doors and windows unlocked at night. Though I had always been curious to see how it had changed, I had no desire to go back there, and should have instructed the driver to take an alternate route. As it turned out, that three-mile journey uptown was one of the most painful trips of my life.

I was finally relieved when the cab pulled up to the curb in front of Joshua Rush's building, and my feet were again on solid ground.

We entered the shiny steel tower along the southwest axis, and followed several signs to the corporate offices of SinStar Technologies. Even though most of the halls were vacant, and we were able to move fairly freely up and down the steps and across the marble floors, surveillance cameras followed our every movement. At the end of the corridor, we paused in front of a pair of massive steel doors. I stared at the reflection of my dark features in the highly-polished surface, and wondered what made Joshua

Rush different from the rest of us. Was it merely the strength of his hired guns, the potency of his addictive drugs, the power of his political connections, or was their something genuinely unique about the man? What twist of fate had placed him in a position of authority while, just a few blocks away, others like him fought it out with automatic weapons for their next meal? Who had made him the head niggah in charge?

As the doors to his office began to open, I turned to my friend. "You realize, of course, that he'll probably have us killed once he gets what he wants. It's not too late to back out."

But Lenny shook his head, more determined than scared to go though with it.

We were soon met by a couple of Rush's men and promptly escorted into his office. Everything in the room was twice as big as necessary. The ceilings were more than twice the height of an average man, and the depth extended more than twice the length of most offices. In the center of the room, an immense conference table towered above several dozen tall chairs. Towards the back, the entire left wall harbored an installation of enormous intricacy. Although far too big and far too involved to take it all in at once, I got an impression of dazzling luminescence from the flashes of light which raced to and fro, seemingly at random, in a constant interchange of energy. When I studied the wall more closely, I saw first a long bank of computers, then a vast complex of monitors, keyboards and laser drives arranged for every conceivable desire, and each one dedicated to a single function. Digital clocks clicked away the seconds, minutes and hours of each major time zone, while a tremendous counter, which stretched from the ceiling to the floor, kept track of changing stock prices one moment to the next. Beyond that, an electronic map of the world's great population centers, divided by corporate boundaries, flashed minute changes in growth and decline. The office was extravagance carried to excess and excess carried to extreme.

While the two of us were being led into this electronic throne room, I couldn't help feeling like some ancient supplicant seeking an audience with the great Caesar himself. Near the back, over-looking a panoramic view of the city, Joshua Rush occupied a tremendous desk which looked more like the control panel of a spacecraft than an office table. Handcrafted from the finest materials, the desk stood taller than anything else in the room. The top rose almost to his shoulders, and surrounded him on three sides with a complex series of dials and switches. He sat back comfortably in a great leather chair, his stubby little legs dangling far above the floor.

The freebooter finally glanced up from one monitor, his forehead beaded with a perspiration which glistened dully in the morning light. "I's been waitin' nearly an hour for you two street punks to sho' up," he bellowed loudly in cityspeak. "I done nearly sent some of the brothers after you, figurin' you had split."

"We got here as quickly as we could."

"Mistah Taylor, time is money. In the fifty-three minutes you's been keepin' me waitin', I done near lost eight thousand dollars—"

I swallowed down a deep gulp, and looked at my friend.

"—eight thousand dollars," he repeated. "Why ain't that nearly the amount I's payin' you?"

"So, send me a bill," I said glibly, not fully realizing what I was saying until well after the words had stumbled off my tongue.

Rush's face instantly hardened. As he regarded me with his dark, lifeless eyes, the beads of sweat on his forehead began dripping down upon the desk. The veins in his neck swelled to nearly bursting, and the pearly white tombstones in his mouth clenched together to the point of nearly crumbling. He then sneered faintly and started to laugh—a long sadistic laugh which carried into the next room. "You damned lucky I got's a sense of humor."

I shivered as a sudden coldness came over my body with the change in his personality, and knew that me and Lenny were in deep shit.

"You doan' like me much, Taylor, do you?" Rush asked after first dismissing his men.

"I hadn't really thought about it, one way or the other."

"Go ahead, admit it. You despise me. You is repulsed by the very notion that this city - your very life - is in the hands of some dumb house niggah?"

"I'm sure you didn't bring us up here just to discuss your popularity quotient," I replied, sidestepping the question, fearing that he was somehow trying to provoke me. "What is it that you want from us?"

"Now, that's what I like—a man who gits right down to the point," he proclaimed, climbing to his feet. Rush tried to hide his annoyance, but I could tell he was pissed off with my tactful evasion. "Do ya know anythin' 'bout stock manipulation or leveraged buyouts?"

"Not very much," I lied.

He typed several commands into his keyboard and a large illuminated display appeared on the wall adjacent to his desk. "This is the market activity for the past seventy-two hours. It s'posed to remain fairly constant to insure economic stability and prevent another recession, but note these surges of transaction." Rush walked around his desk and pointed at the display. He then ran his finger from the top center of one column to the bottom of the next. "That was when the first rumors of a corporate collapse and takeover began—"

"I don't get it."

Joshua Rush looked up with a slight frown. "The point is simple. To control the intire market share, sum'times you must first undermine the confidence investors done got in a single company," he said, bursting with pride. "I started those rumors by sellin' the stocks I own in another company short."

"I still don't understand."

"For over a year now, I's been puttin' the squeeze on GenTech, tryin' to force 'em to sell me controllin' interest. You see, certain parts of the company is worth millions in research and development, while most of the rest is worth shit," he explained. "I want to buy the company out, then sell off the shit; but I can't be doing that as long as I's just a minority stockholder."

"So, what's preventing you from buying up the remaining shares you need to control the company?" I asked, recalling some basic principles of economics. "There must be other investors who want to sell their shares."

"I was doin' just that when GenTech's microcomputah division announced they was on the verge of introducin' a new accelerator chip."

"—and stock transactions froze," I concluded with a simple nod. "But I still don't understand why you would sell your stock at reduced rates when your real goal is to buy the company out."

"To create the illusion of panic," he replied. Rush turned back to the illuminated display and started rearranging columns of figures with an onscreen prompt. "If stock prices start to fall, then others might fear the company is failin' and start sellin' their shares at lower rates as well."

"Of course"—his plan suddenly made sense to me—"then you'd begin buying up all the shares at a rate well below the market value."

The fat man smiled thinly as he wiped the sweat from his forehead with the back of his hand.

"But that ploy can only work if there's evidence of internal problems," I added, "and with so many sophisticated ways of monitoring activities in the matrix, most investors would know, well in advance, that there's nothing wrong."

"Precisely," he said, bored. "That's why I needs someone to enter the matrix and fuck with the company's infrastructure."

"And that's where we come into the picture?"

Rush nodded his head dully.

"But if they already suspect there's a hostile takeover in progress, won't they be protecting their fronts against a possible attack?"

"Course, they will," he responded. "They's not all stupid house niggahs, you know. But they'd never think of protectin' the subsidiaries they rely on for raw materials and technical support."

I had to admit that Joshua Rush's plan was very well conceived. By disrupting the very lifelines that most companies took for granted, he could make it appear that the GenTech Corporation was in financial distress when, in fact, they weren't. Nervous investors would see the value of their shares dwindling, and try to sell the stock off in an effort to avoid their own financial ruin. In the frenzied panic, which would likely follow, Rush could easily reacquire his original shares and purchase the remaining number necessary for controlling interest. He would then dominate the high-tech marketplace with the sale of the new accelerator chip, and make millions by breaking up and selling off the other parts of the company. In another time and place, I might have admired his ruthless approach to corporate warfare, but now my only interest was Lenny's safety. I wondered just how dangerous the interface would be.

While Rush explained in much greater detail what he wanted Lenny to accomplish during the interface, I helped my friend climb into the prosthetic arms and legs of a metallic suit. The suit had been designed as a conduit for the transmission of sensory data to and from the central nervous system of the body. It also helped monitor the electric waves associated with muscle and neuromuscular movements. Because Lenny's system had been so fucked up with the disease, I wasn't certain how effective the equipment would be; but we really didn't have much choice, one way or the other. I took the remaining electrodes from the console and applied them directly to the surface of his face, then activated the electroencephalograph. At least, I'd be able to monitor his brain wave activity with some degree of certainty.

Rush continued laying out his plan, and Lenny listened without interruption or comment, which was strange; he always had hundreds of questions. I didn't know why he was so quiet, and he never told me; but I suspected his mind was focused more on finding Rachel than infiltrating the data banks of the Gen Tech Corporation.

When he finished, Lenny asked, "What type of defensive systems will I be up against?"

"The usual low-level energy weapons," he grunted his answer. Then, after a moment's reflection, Rush added, "They may also be usin' the latest generation of anti-viral drones witch, as ya know, are designed to hunt down and destroy intruders."

"Great!"

"But don't worry," I reassured him. "We'll be able to monitor your movements on the terminal display, and if any thing gets too close, I'll let you know through the comlink. You won't be able to respond to me, but I'll know by your actions that you got my message."

My friend bobbed his head. "What kind of firepower will I be carrying?"

"You'll have the same weapons' systems you had in the 'wars," I replied. "Twin energy pulse canons, which are keyed into your arms and legs, and one thermo-magnetic smart bomb. But remember: don't use that unless you're well out of range of your target."

"I do remember, Jack," he said, with a smirk. "But thanks for reminding me anyway."

"Can we git on with this," Rush said impatiently.

Son of a bitch, I was really starting to get pissed off with that asshole. I shot him a glance, then turned back to Lenny. He seemed to be about as ready as he was ever going to be, and I didn't see a point in delaying the interface any longer. Except to maybe fuck around with that sonuvabitch. I swallowed down a deep gulp of anger, and nodded at him.

Rush leaned over his desk, and removed a small vial of liquid and a syringe from his rather expensive-looking attache case. He filled the syringe with about 30cc of juice, more than enough to send Lenny's metabolism into hyperdrive and help enhance his reaction time. Then, with little concern for my friend's comfort, he jabbed the needle into Lenny's neck, and injected the barbiturate directly into his carotid artery. The drug took affect in no time at all.

Before Lenny was too far gone, I reminded him of a few basic rules. I then carefully fitted the opaque visor over his eyes, which eliminated his vision, and switched on the system. As power moved from the control board into the circuitry of the suit, his hands and feet began to twitch wildly. Soon, his whole body was alive, vibrating with movement. Under the visor, Lenny's face had also changed. Into his features came a deep awareness that seemed to possess only the great thinkers and geniuses of our day. Wiped clean of that foolish grin and infantile stare, his face glowed as though he'd been struck with some final illumination from God.

"Okay, here we go," I spoke into the microphone. "Let's just take it slow until you get reacquainted with the rhythms of your body."

He awkwardly turned thumbs up, then plunged downwards into that bizarre world where the computer data network was a collection of geometric shapes and vast, tortuous landscapes. Most people couldn't handle the sensation of cyberspace, the feeling of weightlessness or tremendous acceleration, the whiplash turns or three hundred-sixty degree loops; others couldn't deal with the visual or auditory input, the large, colorful constructs which raced screaming by at an unbelievable speed. I had tried it myself, and freaked out after less than fifteen seconds. I had become so accustomed, like most people, to the safe brainless activities of virtual reality that real cyberspace scarred the shit out of me. I guess that's what made cyberjocks so special; they weren't afraid to race headfirst on a collision course with ever-changing symbols and images at breakneck speed, and they dared anyone to follow them.

I chose to follow Lenny instead, at a safe distance, on a monitor adjacent to Rush's desk. Displayed on the screen was an electronic schematic of the computer matrix with flashing blips representing each of the major signals. At present, Lenny's signal was the only one of consequence on the screen. But he was far off course, and seemed to be traveling much too slowly.

"What the hell is he doin'?" Joshua Rush exclaimed, with continued impatience. "Those ain't the coordinates I give 'im!"

"Lenny has his own way of doing things," I lied, not quite sure myself.

"Doan' ya fuck with me. I's not some stupid house niggah, you know. I's can read the grid just as well as anyone. Those ain't the coordinates I give 'im!"

"All right, all right. Give me a minute to check in with him and find out—"

But Rush was far too impatient. He engaged the command override, literally taking the control right out of my hands, and started prodding Lenny with an electrical charge. Gently at first, then forcefully, causing his body to jerk back and forth.

"What the hell are you doing?"

"When ya want to move gutter rats, you gots to use a cattle prod," he said coldly.

"You asshole, those electrical pulses are like a signal beacon," I warned him. "Anyone monitoring this portion of the grid is going to know we're there."

Sure enough! No sooner had those words crossed my lips, then two foreign objects appeared in the upper quadrant of the screen. I first thought they were glitches, aberrations, traces of some old, deleted program or simply lost data. But as soon as they began moving toward Lenny's position, I knew they were the anti-viral drones Rush had mentioned.

"Abort, do you read me? Abort!" I yelled into the microphone, but Rush had already cut the output from my headset. I shook it to the floor, and started typing several commands into my keyboard, but he had locked it out as well. "Turn my comlink back on, you sonuvabitch! He's in trouble!"

"He knew the risks," he rumbled softly, though strongly enough to override my demands. His sadistic pleasure, in watching me plead for my friend's life, was evident in the way he savored every syllable. "Besides, I doan' want them tracin' his signal back to me."

"Goddammit, let me help him. He's naked out there without me!"

Rush sat hidden behind the great desk. His flat, hard stare did not once flicker as he pretended that he hadn't quite heard me. Then, the finely chiselled lips parted, and said, "I warn you not to screw this up again." His reply was chilling in its indifference. "Get that fuckin' moron back on course!"

I snapped the headset back into place, and twisted the microphone to my mouth. "Watch your back, buddy; watch your back! You've got two bogeys closing on you from astern."

Lenny's tracking signal went into a steep dive toward one of the thousand geometric constructs, then cut sharply up to avoid detection from the programs below.

"Good move!" I exclaimed.

A series of explosive pulses hopscotched across a large

section of the monitor, leaping from one construct to the next. The blip that represented Lenny had already slipped past the area of the disturbance, but I could tell their probes were not just random, electronic shots in the dark. They were purposely driving him towards GenTech, into some kind of trap.

"They're still right behind you, at about two o'clock," I reported, studying the readouts with care and plotting his next possible move, "but I don't think they've locked onto your signal yet. You may still be able to shake them off by turning to grid reference 21-87-4. Whatever you do, stay away from those relays."

On the monitor, Lenny's signal skimmed daringly close to GenTech's master control program, narrowly missing one of the two relay towers, his attention seemingly trained over his shoulder on the distant drones. Had the surface installations seen him? I wasn't really sure. Perhaps they were simply programmed to return fire, and had no real offensive capabilities? I couldn't take that chance, and warned him away from the construct. I had hoped he would return to the open course, where he'd at least have a running chance; but instead he accelerated towards the surface, whipping past the other towering dataliths. Electronic crosshairs zeroed on his signal, and instantly he was enveloped in a mesh-work of energy pulses and plasma beams.

"Get out of there! They're got a weapon's lock on you. Move!!!!" I glanced away from the monitor and watched his body jerk back and forth, his arms raised in defensive posture.

The enemy stations continued to hammer away, successive bolts flashing near him. Each electrical pulse carried enough mega-wattage to destroy even the most complex virus, and if Lenny wasn't careful, his mind would end up fried like an egg on the griddle. The plasma beams were far worse, though; one hit and his whole body would turn into a conduit for disaster, unleasing a chain-reaction which could destroy the whole system. But I was certain Rush would pull the plug long before that.

Twisting, spinning, diving, Lenny looped back toward the relays, and accelerated through another whiplash turn. He wove a tight path around the protruding towers, in an obvious move to draw the deadly fire on the master control program itself, all to no avail. As his signal approached the twin constructs, the surface installations ceased firing upon him.

During that momentary lull, I scanned the monitor for the two drones. They were crossing the lower portion of the screen, their small dark signals closing with ruthless determination. They had finally locked onto his position, and would not stop until his signal had been terminated. Closer and closer, they moved. They were as implacable as the predatory creatures that roamed the streets at night, with cruel mouths open, looking for their next meal. Closer. Their swollen tongues licking razor-sharp teeth in anticipation of the kill. Closer. Now Lenny had only seconds to react, seconds to arm and target his weapons. Only seconds to . . .

"Fire!" I shouted, and in that very instant, the screen exploded with a brilliant flash of light.

Lenny was thrown heavily back against the console, and collapsed to the floor. As he lay there on his back, still sealed in the suit but safe from the ravages of that other world, his whole body began to vibrate. First his hands and feet, then his entire arms and legs, and finally his whole body. He clenched his teeth and gave a loud, gasping cry, while hammering his head against the floor in a strange rhythmic motion.

I hastily slipped both hands under his head and pulled him into my lap. Lenny inhaled deeply and let out an unearthly howl that made Rush jump, then he fell silent in my arms. "Can't you see he's having a seizure," I snapped. "Get a doctor in here, you sonuvabitch. Now!"

The fat man started to say something, hesitated, then shock his head in disgust. "Fuckin' amateurs!" he sneered, lumbering from the room.

"Hurry," I added, but he was already gone.

*   *   *   *   *

Within a short period of time, my unconscious friend was stirring and mumbling like a dreaming sleeper. "Rachel . . . Rachel . . .Rachel. . ."

"Take it easy, buddy. Relax," I said, still craddling him like a child.

Lenny gradually opened his eyes and stared straight forward, like he was still asleep. As the vagueness began to disappear, his eyes brightened—first in wonder, then in exaltation, and finally ecstacy. He gave a shout of pure joy, "Rachel!"

"No," I replied, trying to ease his disappointment with a reassuring smile. "I'm sorry, Lenny. It's just me, your friend Jack."

Lenny's head came up, and he glanced around the room with vacant eyes. No, not quite vacant... There was something burning in the back of them—something that I simply could not describe. Without a word, he threw off my hands and climbed to a sitting position. He then carefully reexamined the contours of the room, taking in every nook and shadow. His gaze finally came back to me. "She was here, Jack. I know she was here."

"Calm down, buddy. Try to relax. You've just suffered a tremendous shock."

"But I heard her whispering, calling my name."

I rose to my feet and wandered to the edge of the room in search of Joshua Rush. Where the hell was that doctor he had promised? What was taking him so long? Lenny might have already croaked for all he'd known; unless, of course, Rush had never intended to call for a doctor. The cost and publicity, after all, might have been more than what he had bargained for.

Turning, I looked back over my shoulder and studied the painful expression in Lenny's face. He had gotten over his seizure, but I could tell that he was still pretty weak. There was also that vacant look of desperation in his eyes, that loss of hope which I had seen hundreds of times in the street. He appeared like someone who had finally reached the edge and was about to plunge to his death.

Lenny sank deep into despair, like a drowning man in a river. After a while, though, my friend stirred, evidently having reached some great plateau of understanding. "I've got to go back in."

"Are you crazy? You nearly got yourself killed during the last interface—"

"But don't you see. That's what she was trying to tell me," he declared with deceptive coolness, a slight glimmer of hope returning to his vacant eyes. "Rachel didn't come back with me because she's made a place for us there, on the farside."

"Rachel is dead," I repeated for the umpteenth time.

"No, she isn't, Jack," he insisted. "The part of her that I love is still very much alive."

"I'm not going to let you do this."

"Trust me. I know what I'm doing."

As I watched him climb awkwardly back into position, I felt powerless to do anything. He wanted that dream more than life itself, and who was I to stand in his way. "You stupid fool, you're going to kill yourself," I tried reasoning with him one last time.

Lenny acknowledged my concern with a nod. "How much longer you think I've I got? A month? Two months? I can't quit now that I'm so close."

"Stop talking nonsense. We're getting out of here--together!"

"No, not this time," he returned. Then, after a moment of silent reflection, my friend added, "You've got your whole life ahead of you. Take the money and made a fresh start with it."

"God, after all these years, I wouldn't know what to do by myself."

"Dream," he said simply.

"I've always relied on you for my dreams. What am I going to do when you're no longer here?"

"Jack, you're not talkin' me out of this."

"But what about Rush?"—I was now grasping at straws—"When he comes back in, and finds that you've gone, he'll probably kill me."

"Don't worry," he calmly replied. "I'll fix it so that Rush never bothers you again."

"No," I choked, "forget it. It's far too risky! Let's just get the hell out of here, and take our chances on the street."

"Goodbye, Jack," he whispered faintly. "Rachel and I will never forget you."

I reached down to touch his forehead, but already he was fading away, blending back into the equipment. Crying out, I clawed desperately for his mechanical hand. But as his fingers closed one final time in the glove of the prosthesis, he was gone.

I looked down at my friend, and in the instant before he passed onto the other side, I could see a faint smile cross his face. He hadn't smiled in years, and yet it was one of those rare smiles, with a quality of eternal reassurance in it, that you may come across four or five times in life.

Within seconds, the room was clamoring with a shrill, whooping siren—loud enough to draw that fat sonuvabitch back from his outer office. Mere heartbeats later, Rush came racing into the room to discover his vast complex of computers was building to an overload, but it was far too late to do anything. The hum rose to a roar. A drift of smoke wafted up from a one of the terminals. Then a shower of sparks burst from one of the machine's metallic faces -and with a blast of exploding circuits, all the lights went out and systems came crashing down.

He watched in horror as the large illuminated display of his stock holdings faded into obscurity.

His hands began to tremble, and for the first time the look of fear came across Rush's face. In that instant, I realized what it was that set him apart from others, and I was no longer afraid. The worst he could do was kill me, and with Lenny gone, that would have been more a blessing than a threat.

"What the fuck have you done?" he whimpered repeatedly in disbelief. "What the fuck have you done?"

I shrugged, far too exhausted to care. "Figure it out yourself, Rush."

He looked at me fiercely; his dark, lifeless eyes had turned blood red. "My money . . . my holdin's . . . my power. Your incompetance has done cost me everythin'. Everythin'!"

"Everything?" I repeated, with mock concern.

Joshua Rush bounded across the floor, and dragged me from the workstation. I grabbed feebly at his wrists, but his massive hands had already tightened around my throat. When he lifted me into the air, my arms and legs flopped helplessly, like a rag doll. The fat man then pulled me closer, panting. "You little prick, who the hell do you think you're fuckin' with here?"

"Some dumb house niggah," I gasped.

Rush stared into my eyes. "I owns half of the banks, businesses, and housing in this city. I also control most of the illegal drugs, gambling and prostitution," he snarled. "Did you really think you could fuck with me and get away with it?"

I opened my mouth to answer him, but the words were choked off by his contracting fingers.

He threw me backwards. I thudded against the wall, and collapsed to the floor. Rush then stood over me, his sweating face fiendish under the dull office lights. I felt a hard kick in the ribs, and groaned. The foot again smashed into my body. He kicked me again and again and again. "You're a dead man," he said finally. "When the brothers git through messin' wit'cho, you's going to beg them to kill you."

I tasted blood in my mouth. "Not man enough to do it yourself, huh?"

Rush raised his fists into the air, hesitated for a moment, then lowered them to his side. "Get the fuck out of here, you little cockroach!" he blustered with anger. "You gots forty-eight hours to get the fuck out of my town! After that, I's going to have you hunted down and killed like a dog."

Painfully, I dragged myself to my knees, and looked up at him with an equal measure of confusion and contempt. Why was he letting me go free? What could he possibly loose from killing some gutter rat like me? It then dawned on me that Rush must have feared me, and what the implications of my death might mean to authorities now that he was no longer as well connected, far worse than I had ever feared him. Or, maybe it was even much simpler than that. Perhaps, for the first time in his life, somebody had stood up to him, and like that school yard bully, he collapsed in fear. I didn't know, and I was certainly not going to stick around his offices to find out.

I went into hiding, burrowing deep into that strange world where transients, privateers, criminals, derelicts and the other dregs of the earth hid. But the sonuvabitch never did come looking for me.

After eating dirt for six months, I learned that Joshua Rush had been arrested for insider trading, then slain in prison by a rival gang member while awaiting trial. News accounts also revealed that his fat, overweight body had snatched from the morgue by hungry predators in a daring night raid. I wasn't very surprised, but I did give up meat for awhile and became a vegetarian.

When I finally did leave Central City, I headed for the West Coast with thoughts of starting over in San Francisco or New Tokyo. Along the way, I stopped off in Glenwood Springs, Colorado, to erect a marker next to Doc Holiday's gravestone in memory of my friend. Lenny would have never appreciated the subtle irony in that gesture, but I'm sure he would have approved. In New Tokyo, I invested our money in the GenTech Corporation, with the knowledge that they were on the verge of releasing a new accelerator chip, and made a fortune on the deal. Well, at least enough to live the rest of my life in comfort . . .

Twenty years have passed since then, and I still recall those events as if they had happened yesterday. I guess that's one reason why I decided to write them down at last, to put them to rest. I think about my friend quite often, too, and wonder if I will ever meet another person like him. He had such an extraordinary gift for hope, a belief in the promises of life that transcend the commonplace, and in the end I think he found his dream.

He taught me that fear makes most men impotent and that hope allows others to dream. I guess, somewhere in the middle, the rest of us survive.

Satisfaction Guaranteed

Like most college students of my generation, I worked my way through school. I did not qualify for scholarships or financial aid, and declined military service, due in large part to an undeclared war in Southeast Asia. With opportunities quite limited, I went to work at Sears, Roebuck and Company. I worked for Sears as a salesman in the young men's clothing department for five years, while I struggled to get my Bachelor's and Master's Degrees. The work itself wasn't really hard, except perhaps at Christmas or during the Back-to-School rush, and the customers were generally very pleasant. Every so often, however, the customer from hell would arrive to torment and terrorize us. "Satisfaction Guaranteed" is dedicated to those customers from hell.

"Listen," the Time Traveler said to the salesrobot at the customer service desk in the Sears & Roebuck store on Mars, "I just purchased this sonic screwdriver about thirteen seconds ago, and I'm not entirely satisfied with its operation."

"What seems to be the problem, sir?" the salesrobot inquired.

"If you don't mind, I was here first!" the eight-foot tall, green-skinned, tentacled alien exclaimed, shoving her mechanical monstrosity between the Time Traveler and the customer service desk.

The Time Traveler merely nodded.

"I bought this robot dressmaker six light years ago, when it was on sale," she explained, pointing to the monstrosity, "and I distinctly remember telling the salesrobot that I wanted the atomic-powered model. But apparently, he was too busy talking to the water cooler, and made the mistake of wrapping this solar-powered one instead. Do you have an idea how I'm supposed to use a solar-powered dressmaker out on Uranus? We barely get enough light to power the coffeemaker."

"Yes, madam," the robot sighed.

"Well, I have been shopping at Sears for many years," she

continued, "and I have always had the satisfaction of your products and services guaranteed. But lately, it has been a disgrace!"

The Time Traveler groaned, glancing at his chronometer.

"As a customer, I feel that I have the right to prompt, courteous attention," she added, browbeating the robot behind the customer service desk, "but I feel that right has been thoroughly denied to me. After all, I had to make a special trip here, just to return this item." The eight-foot-tall, green-skinned, tentacled alien snatched the plaque with the company motto from the wall with one tentacle, and shoved it under the salesrobot's nose with another. "Your sign does say, 'Satisfaction guaranteed, or--'"

"Yes, madam, you are absolutely right," the salesrobot replied.

"Kindly refrain from interrupting me when I am speaking!" she exclaimed, hurling the sign away in anger. "You are a very rude robot, and now I demand to speak to your superior immediately!"

The salesrobot nodded, then pressed a small red button in front of him. Instantly, the eight-foot-tall, green-skinned, tentacled alien was vaporized into a cloud of thick smoke.

"Now, sir," the robot asked, "how can I serve you?"

The Time Traveler stared back through the cloud at the customer service desk, his eyes nearly popping out of his head. He took two steps backwards, and turned to run, as fast as his feet would carry him, back to his time machine.

"Sir, we do guarantee satisfaction," the salesrobot said, removing the mechanical monstrosity of a dressmaker from the sales floor.

"Well, I may have been mistaken—"

"Please, let me assist you," the robot persisted.

The Time Traveler took a deep gulp of air, then placed the item on the customer service desk. "As I explained before, I just purchased this sonic screwdriver. I had to make a few emergency repairs to my time machine, but I wasn't entirely satisfied with the screwdriver's performance."

The salesrobot nodded. "Would you like a replacement, sir? Or would you prefer a refund?"

"A replacement would be fine," he said, tentatively.

The robot again nodded, then pushed a series of buttons in front of him. Instantly, a replacement for the sonic screwdriver appeared on the desk. The salesrobot picked it up, and handed it to the Time Traveler.

"Thank you, sir," the robot added, "please come again."

Confused, the Time Traveler shook his head, and walked away from the customer service desk, repeating to himself, "Satisfaction guaranteed . . ."

Solutions

"Solutions" takes place in a parallel universe where the world's greatest detective doesn't have all of the answers, and the solution to the mystery—which is the granddaddy of all mysteries—comes from a most unusual source. Or does it? I had a great deal of fun writing this story in the style and diction of Sir Arthur Conan Doyle, attempting to capture the nuances of the character of Sherlock Holmes through the first-person narrative of Dr. John H. Watson. Pastiches of Sherlock Holmes stories are almost as old as the original canon, but in recent years, these loving and sincere imitations have explored aspects of the great detective's character never before imagined. For example, in The Seven Percent Solution, *Nicholas Meyer examined Holmes' cocaine addiction. Here, Holmes faces a truly bizarre case.*

During my long and intimate acquaintance with Sherlock Holmes, I had never once considered the inner workings of his soul. I had always thought of him as a brain without a heart, an unemotional character with an aversion to women and a disinclination to form new friendships. But a few short months after my marriage, he seemed to grow even more distant, isolated, as if caught in the throes of some vexatious problem. And I, in my limited capacity as a general practitioner and consulting physician, felt my friend found my services inadequate.

Less than a fortnight later, I received a telegram from Holmes requesting my medical services. I need not say that my eyes had hardly glanced over the paper before I sprang into a hansom cab and was on my way to my old residence at 221B Baker Street.

* * * * *

Upon arrival, I hurried up the stairs and stole into his darkened room. He was huddled in his armchair, and I heard my name in a hoarse whisper. The blind was three-quarters down, but a ray of street light slanted through and struck his crimson wound. I sat beside him and carefully touched his injury with a white linen compress.

"All right, Watson. Don't look so scared," he muttered in a very low voice. "It's not as bad as it seems. A lacerated scalp wound and a few bruises. Kindly give me a shot of morphine to ease the pain—"

"Holmes, how did it happen?" I cried with an immense sigh of amazement as I readied the needle.

"A night stalker. An assassin!" he remarked, grimacing with the pain. "It happens that I was engaged in an investigation of the murder of Madame Montpensier for her sister when I struck from behind by an assassin."

"An assassin?" I asked. "What reason would an assassin have to kill you?"

"That we may never know, Watson," said my companion, with a somewhat bitter frown. Sherlock Holmes sat silent for a few moments with his brows knitted and his eyes fixed on the street. "I took him off guard by turning his second blow back upon him. We struggled, fighting for control of his weapon. We fell, he upon the blade and I was shook up by no worse than you see me now. I staggered away, leaving him for dead."

I shook my head gravely, carefully injecting my friend with the morphine.

"Thank you, my dead friend," Holmes replied at last, glancing away from the needle. Then, a few moments later, he was scribbling a few notes on a half sheet of paper. "Perhaps we can discover the identity and motive of the assassin from the evidence at hand—"

"Good gracious, Holmes!" I shouted. "You've just narrowly escaped an assassin's blade and all you can think about is crime and deduction!"

"Consider the details," he observed, taking up his long cherrywood pipe and lighting it with his characteristically bent match. "Madame Montpensier was stabbed to death in her second story flat one block away from my attack. The Yard informed me that her assailant had entered through an open window and that both she and her unborn child were victims of his blade. Now, first of all, presuming the assassin had a purpose, what could he gain from the murder of a pregnant woman, or a consulting detective?"

"Holmes, what makes you think—" I scowled, putting aside my medical bag. "—that there's a connection between her murder and your—"

As I spoke, there was a sudden tap at the door, followed by Mrs. Hudson announcing a female visitor. Sherlock Holmes welcomed her with an outstretched hand and, having signaled Mrs. Hudson away, he introduced Miss Virginia Elridge to me and offered her an armchair.

"I owe you an apology for intruding like this," she said. "I came to talk in more detail about my sister, but I didn't know you had company."

Holmes shook his head. "Not at all," he remarked. "Dr. Watson is my friend and partner."

"I have heard, Mr. Holmes," Miss Eldridge stated, "that you can solve any mystery—"

"Indeed?" he replied.

"—and that you have never been beaten?"

Sherlock Holmes grinned indulgently, withdrawing his pipe. "I have been beaten four times," he said. "Three times by men, and once by a woman."

"Oh?"

"Please continue."

"I have been riding in a coach from Devonshire all afternoon," she replied, sitting forward in her chair, "hoping that you had learned something about my sister's death."

"Miss Eldridge," I interrupted with an impatient gasp, "my friend was almost skilled tonight by an assassin's blade while investigating that murder, and . . ."(turning my gaze towards him) "he should be resting!"

"Oh, Mr. Homes, I didn't—"

But Holmes remained undaunted, shaking his head and scribbling a few more notes. He then sank deep into his chair and persisted in his investigation by requesting further details surrounding the murder.

"I do not know exactly where to begin, Mr. Holmes, so my narrative may seem rather disjointed," she explained. "My sister has been a widow for two years now, and life in general has not been very kind to her. Several months ago, I received a letter from her detailing a liaison with a most distinguished gentleman. She told him that his name was H. Wesley Chesterfield, that he had called upon her for several evenings over a fortnight, and that he had purchased several expensive gifts for her. I was naturally envious of her good fortune until I learned that Chesterfield was already married and had fathered two sons."

"Was your sister aware of his particular station in life?" I asked.

"My sister was not a tramp, Dr. Watson, if that's what you are implying," she objected, folding her arms in defense. "Her involvement with Chesterfield was handled with dignity and utmost discretion!"

I shrugged and shot a questioning glance at my companion.

"Please continue, Miss Eldridge," Holmes insisted.

The woman nodded, then with great hesitation, said, "I was upon receipt of her second letter that I became most concerned. She wrote that he had secured apartments for her, requesting that she receive no visitors and that she not leave during the day. His insistence upon these two points seemed most peculiar, and it was at that point when I decided to pay her a visit.

"I can well remember driving up to her house in the evening, some three weeks before the fatal event. She was standing in the window when I stepped from the cab. I waved to her—but her eyes seemed fixed on something beyond me with an expression of dreadful horror. I turned around and had just enough time to catch a glimpse of H. Wesley Chesterfield, lurking in the shadows.

"I stayed with my sister the rest of the evening," she continued. "She seemed terribly upset, and she confided with me that she was pregnant with Chesterfield's child. She also feared that he would kill her. This may be insignificant but there is the missing locket he gave her with the picture of him. Underneath the picture is a some strange date and address."

Sherlock Holmes sat up in his chair. "That is where our connection lies, Watson," he said, mystifying both of us. "Can you describe this Chesterfield for us?"

"I really only saw him for an instant, Mr. Holmes," Miss Eldridge replied. "He was a rather large gentleman in his late fifties with a receding hair line—"

Sherlock Holmes stood up and walked across the room.

"That is most interesting," said my companion sourly, folding his notes and placing them gingerly into his pocket.

"What is it, Holmes?" I inquired.

"God help us!" said Holmes after a long silence. "Why does fate play such tricks with us? I have never heard of such a case as this! Your description of Chesterfield, Miss Eldridge, matches that of the assassin who attacked me. And yet, it seems all too easy—"

"Bravo, Holmes," I shouted. "You have solved the mystery."

"There is no mystery, Watson," he interposed, "when the circumstances become so easily unwound."

The lady stood up and crossed the floor to Holmes. "I appreciate your time and patience, and I regret that you were injured while investigating my unfortunate sister's demise."

My companion merely nodded to her.

"But I am quite satisfied that her murderer rots in the deepest bowels of the earth," Miss Virginia Eldridge added with vehemence.

Sherlock Holmes raised his dark eyebrows, smiled, and shook her hand. He then walked her to the door and requested a cab take her home.

Once the lady had departed, I approached my friend and said, "I am somewhat confused, Holmes. Why—"

"I grow weary of questions, Watson," he stated elusively, lighting a candle and walking to his bedroom. "No doubt the morphine has made me drowsy. Be good enough to lock the door on your way out."

*   *   *   *   *

The following morning, I was in my dressing gown, reading the Daily Telegraph, when I next saw Sherlock Holmes. I heard a tap at the door, and my good friend entered. The depressed look was no longer on his face, and from his pocket he withdrew a small piece of paper. He unfolded the paper and read it aloud:

"Come instantly, 425 Farthington Street, Westminster. Inspector Lestrade."

"What do you think it is?" I asked.

"I don't know, Watson," my companion replied. "Things have been rather quiet down at the Yard, and I haven't read about any misdoings in the newspaper. Unless—" Holmes paused for a moment, holding the piece of paper in the air, "—this has something to do with—"

"—Chesterfield?"

"Quickly, Watson," cried Sherlock Holmes, "the game is afoot!"

*   *   *   *   *

In a half an hour our hansom pulled up in front of the address on the paper. The setting was a heavily timbered park which, stretching up a gentle slope, thickened into a grove at the highest point. From amid the branches, I could see the gray gables and high roof of a very old mansion.

Sherlock Holmes paid the hansom driver, then turned his attention towards the house.

Inspector Lestrade hurried forward to meet us with a face which spoke his relief. "I've been waiting anxiously for you," he said, shaking hands with us warmly. "I need your help, Holmes, in clearing up some minor details in a murder investigation. How much do you know about an H. Wesley Chesterfield?"

My companion winced slightly. "All too much."

Inspector Lestrade took out his official notebook and glanced through the pages. "H. Wesley Chesterfield, a prominent retainer, was stabbed to death—"

"That much I know!" exclaimed Holmes abruptly.

"—and his body was discovered," Lestrade continued, "by one of his servants in his study this morning."

"What?" I cried, looking quickly to my friend.

"Impossible!" Holmes insisted. "Shortly after twilight, Chesterfield attacked me several block from here, and I was forced to kill him with his own knife."

"Are you certain of this, Holmes?" Lestrade inquired, re-checking his notes.

"Yes," he replied.

"I intended his wounds after his unfortunate enough," I added.

"Then someone is lying," the Inspector stated, looking at his notebook. He closed it in frustration and pointed to the house. "We already had a prime suspect in custody down at the Yard."

"Miss Virginia Eldridge," said Holmes.

"Yes, the servants identified her as the last person to see—" Lestrade continued, reaching for the doorbell. He then paused and looked at my companion. "How did you know we had Miss Eldridge in custody?"

Before Sherlock Holmes could respond, one of Chesterfield's servants met us at the door and explained that he had been waiting for us. The servant led us down a short passage and up a flight of stairs, which ended at a door. He opened it and showed us Chesterfield's body.

"Clutching a volume of Greek tragedy. Really!" I protested. "A bit overly melodramatic, wouldn't you say, Holmes?"

"That is certainly very novel," he observed.

"*Oedipus Tyrannus* by Sophocles," Inspector Lestrade read the title as he removed the book from Chesterfield's fingers. "This could have some meaning."

Sherlock Holmes shook his head impatiently. "A dying clue? Really, Lestrade."

"A tray of bent matches—"

"Chesterfield may have been a pipe smoker," Holmes replied with some irritation. "Consider all the evidence, Lestrade, coldly and objectively."

I looked curiously at the two detectives as they argued the obvious clues, then addressed myself to the body of H. Wesley Chesterfield. A superficial examination of the corpse told me that he had been stabbed once in the lower abdomen; but upon closer analysis, I noted a bad bruise on his forehead, which might suggest that he had struggled with his assailant before he died. I unbuttoned his shirt and began to examine the body.

"Holmes, look at this," I said, pulling out a chain and locket. "The missing locket of which Miss Eldridge spoke. Look under the picture is the date January 6, 1854, and the name Quinland House, North Riding."

"Interesting," remarked Holmes.

"Now, Holmes—" I demanded, snapping to my feet.

Sherlock Holmes put a finger to his lips and glanced at me. "All of this is very elementary, Watson," he said to me. "I find nothing here of any consequence."

"But what about the dying clue?" I inquired, hoping to calm the detective from Scotland Yard. "What of the volume of Sophocles?"

"It is interesting that both you and Lestrade brought that to my attention," he remarked. "*Oedipus Tyrannus* by Sophocles is the classic detective story of a young king who learns he has murdered his father and slept with his mother."

"What relevance could that story have to this case?" I queried the Great Detective.

"Precisely, Watson," he said. "Clues which have no meaning, and a dead body which miraculously reappears here in this study."

I stared at the body in astonishment, then began rummaging through his pockets. I felt that there had to be at least one piece of conclusive evidence.

Holmes was about to make another observation when a rather guant-looking gentleman, dressed in professional robes, entered the room. He quickly surveyed the body, paused for a moment of grief, and then turned questioningly to the three of us.

"I am Henry Chesterfield," he said in whispered silence. "He was my father, and I only received notice of his death an hour ago."

"His son!" Lestrade grunted his pleasure. "Where were you last night?" he demanded, instantly drawing his notebook and assuming control of the situation.

"I was at the University—"

"The University," he repeated.

"—teaching a course in Greek drama," Henry Chesterfield reported. "I am an associate professor of classical studies--"

Lestrade interrupted, "The dying clue."

Sherlock Holmes smiled demurely.

"Certainly you cannot suspect me of his murder?"

"I'll ask the questions, Chesterfield," declared Lestrade, in his best bullying voice. "How would you characterize your relationship with your father? Did he agree with your political views and recognize your station in life? Did you often quarrel or publicly."

"Lestrade, it is obvious that this man is innocent," said my companion finally.

The Inspector gave an ejaculation of impatience. "If you don't mind, Holmes, I'll conduct this investigation without your help."

Sherlock Holmes paused for a moment, then shook his head. "When will you learn, Lestrade, that detection is an exacting science?" he scowled. "This man is clearly innocent! There are no scars of bruises on his person, and I believe if you check his story, you will find that his students corroborate his alibi."

"Well done, Holmes!" I exclaimed.

Professor Henry Chesterfield stepped past Lestrade and shook hands with my companion. "You must be Sherlock Holmes?" he asked. "I would be greatly in your debt if you could learn the identity of my father's murderer."

"My regrets on the loss of your father," Holmes said, turning to leave. "Come along, Watson."

Lestrade caught my friend by the shoulder. "Virginia Eldridge," he said slowly, "must be the murderer."

Holmes shook his head negatively.

"And why is she innocent?"

"She had the motive, Lestrade," Sherlock Holmes reported, "but she had neither the opportunity nor design to commit murder. In point of fact, I believe she came up here yesterday with the intention of murdering H. Wesley Chesterfield, but she lost her nerve."

"There are no other suspects, Holmes!" Lestrade cried in despair.

"Not so," I said hesitantly.

Lestrade pricked up his ears.

"I think I have the solution to the mystery," I replied coolly, quietly examining the locket. "I will reveal the identity of the murderer as soon as I have completed one final errand."

*   *   *   *   *

I left Lestrade and Holmes in a state of utter confusion, but I had my reasons. Through the evidence, I had deduced the identity of the murderer, and I hope that my final inquiries would validate my solution to the mystery.

Those final inquiries took me first to the registrar of county records in Yorkshire. And upon receiving verification of the birth certificate and land lease, I then paid a visit on Mycroft Holmes at the Diogenes Club. My last stop was Swamdam Mortuary in the Southern most part of London.

By the time I arrived there, the sun had set, and an eerie fog enshrouded the setting. I did not often frequent charnel houses at night, but it was essential that I examine Madame Montpensier's body before it was entombed.

I approached the alley door with extreme caution and vigilance. Finding it unattended, I slipped in and paused quietly in the open door.

Through the gloom, I could dimly glimpse the bodies lying in strange and fantastic poses—bowed shoulders, bent knees, heads thrown back and chins pointing upward, with here and there a dark lackluster eye turned in my direction. Out of the black shadows, a light glimmered through the corpses. Knowing that it was not the attendant, I assumed the murderer had anticipated my move.

I walked down the narrow passage between the double row of cadavers, holding my breath to keep out the vile, stupefying stench of death, and then paused to look about for the light. It was several paces still in front of me, and I could almost make out the murderer's face. I took two forward steps and stumbled, head first, into the upraised palms of a badly disfigured corpse. I cried out in horror, and by doing so, made my presence known.

The murderer hesitated for a long silent moment and stepped into the light.

I rose to my feet, stared at him for several seconds in utter astonishment, and then it appears that I must have fainted from the strain. Certainly, a grey mist swirled before my eyes, and when it cleared, I found my collarends undone and my friend Sherlock Holmes attending me.

"My dear Watson," said Holmes, "I owe you an apology for startling you like that. I thought that you were, perhaps, the murderer. I had no idea that—"

I gripped him by the arm.

"Holmes!" I cried, straightening myself up. "What are earth are you doing here?"

"Madame Montpensier's murder," he explained, resuming his investigation of the mortuary. "I must confess, Watson, that this case has me baffled, and I was hoping that a re-examination of the body would provide some additional information. I can't help thinking that I've overlooked something. There must be a connection—"

"Holmes!" I declared. "I know how the murderer is."

"Excellant, Watson!" exclaimed Sherlock Holmes, focusing his magnifying glass on me. "Then you must have found the connecting thread!"

I nodded and replied, "The connection, Holmes, is one of coincidence. Nothing more! But it did lead me to one inescapable conclusion."

"What are you saying, Watson?"

"You murdered H. Wesley Chesterfield," said I.

"Elementary, my dear Watson," he replied. "You already have my confession of the incidents that occurred last evening, and you know of my employment by Miss Virginia Eldridge."

"Yes, Holmes," I answered. "But where in fact did those incidents take place?"

Sherlock Holmes looked grave.

"You met with Chesterfield yesterday afternoon," I suggested, stepping closer to him, "disguised, just as you've done on numerous occasions, as a woman. As Miss Virginia Eldridge."

"But what reason would I have to kill Chesterfield?" he protested.

"You probably confronted him with the locket, which you discovered in the Madame Montpensier investigation," I replied, "and insisted that he had killed not only her, but also your real mother!"

"That's preposterous!" he shouted.

"I thought so, too, until I re-examined the documents at the registrar in Yorkshire," I explained, "and spoke with your brother Mycroft at the Diogenes Club. He contends that you are only his adopted brother.''

Holmes shook his head in confusion.

"The solution to the mystery became all too clear when I compared it with the similar, unfortunate case of Madame Montpensier." I withdrew the locket and handed it to my clever companion. "From this, I discovered a most bizarre and tragic story: In the year 1863, H. Wesley Chesterfield rented a house at North Riding in Yorkshire, with the sole purpose of hiding his mistress from polite society.

"After a year of secret residence, the young woman, to Chesterfield's exasperation, gave birth to an infant son. The date of birth, January 6, 1854, was certified by the attending midwife. Days after the birth, Chesterfield took the woman's life and put the infant in a cloth, burying both bodies in an alleyway by the side of the house. This ungodly act was witnessed from an upper window of the house by a servant. He disinterred the bodies and, discovering the child was still alive, carried it to the safety of a previous employer. A person with whom you are quite familiar—Sigerson Holmes."

Holmes was profoundly silent.

"However," I continued, "the specific details did not come together until I realized that it was no accident that he died clutching the volume of Sophocles. Chesterfield was determined to leave us a clue as to the identity of his assailant."

"The dying clue," he gasped.

"Yes, the tragic tale of a detective who learns that he has committed the murder."

Sherlock Holmes sank, his face in his hands.

I unbuttoned my collarends, returned the locket to my pocket, and reached out for him. "I am terribly sorry, my dear friend, but there is only one possible solution to the mystery."

"Not so, Watson," he retorted with an expression of resolve. "There is an alternative solution. **There must be!**"

Count on Doomsday

Count Dracula represents one of the most important archetypes of Victorian literature; he is the quintessential Byronic hero who never quite made the transition to postmodern society and culture. He is the embodiment of romanticism, immortality, and sexuality, and Bram Stoker's original novel brilliantly explores that unknown territory of his soul where love, imagination, and mutual satisfaction become sex, fantasy, dominance, submission, and degradation of the spirit. In writing "Count on Doomsday," I was not interested in going back over the familiar ground which so many of my contemporaries had covered; but rather, I wanted to explore how this typically Victorian character would survive in a brave, new, atomic world.

Count Dracula, the last surviving vampire, awoke on the day after the atomic war and discovered, much to his horror, that he was alone.

Dust particles and radioactive debris had filled the sky, blotting out the harmful rays of the sun, as perpetual midnight enshrouded the Earth. He watched as the dark clouds linked to form a vast canopy overhead, then shivered as the cold wind of the nuclear winter spread its snowy fall-out. He was finally freed to move about in the day-time, but that was of little comfort now. He faced, for the first time in his life, starvation and loneliness. His species was a superior one, evolving independently of mankind, and had been content merely to feed upon humanity like cattle. There was never a need to rule, dominate, or destroy fellow members of his race. Throughout the centuries, his ancestors had survived the Flood, the Inquisition, and two world wars, had flourished during the Dark Ages, and had out-lived many tyrants and kings. He himself had once been a king, and as Vlad the Impaler he had sent nearly 20,000 people to their deaths. But in this brave, new century of push-button wars and rampant technology, the power of the vampire had gone out of the world. Pollution, drug use and disease had contaminated the purity of the blood, and one-by-one his species had died out. He was the last of his kind.

With much difficulty, Dracula struggled to his feet and climbed from his coffin. He stood silently inside his burial vault and surveyed his immediate surroundings. The finely etched, marble walls and ceiling of the crypt had collapsed around him. His red velvet curtains - once plush and stately - had disintegrated to ash, and his coat-of-arms and twin-dragon statues - symbols of his royal heritage - had melted into a mass of blackened metal. Only the vault's heavy iron doors remained. Greatly saddened, Dracula stepped outside into the darkness.

He paused at the vault's threshold, closing the doors behind him, and then looked across the wasteland in disbelief. The city of New York, once a metropolis of excitement and beauty, was now an enormous cemetary; the tall, gray buildings, broken and overturned, stood as silent monuments in that vast graveyard. Between Fifth Avenue and 72nd Street, there was a large black crater which had been formed by the ground-burst of a one-megaton bomb. Nearby, the narrow streets were littered with wrecked cars, smoldering fires, shattered glass, and building debris. Slumped in the East River, the Brooklyn Bridge was a twisted pile of planks and girders. In the distance, Lady Liberty, her copper skin burned off by the explosive fire-ball, now stood as a skeleton at the mouth of New York harbor, while images of anxious tourists were charred in silhouette at the base of her monument. And all across the cityscape, as far as his eyes could see, there were millions of unburied corpses, looking despairingly to him for their ultimate salvation.

Dracula refused to accept his fate, and reassured himself that someone must have survived.

Venturing into the city, Count Dracula searched desperately for some sign of life. But death and destruction was all that awaited him. As he wandered through the streets, he witnessed many scenes of unspeakable horror, and slowly he began to accept the truth. Then, at Radio City Music Hall, Dracula discovered the remains of a typical family - husband, wife, and two children - as they stood waiting for tickets that they would never use. Their skeletons - though stripped of flesh and blood - seemed perfectly preserved, but when he bent down to touch one of the children, its hollow figure crumbled into a fine, powdered dust.

As he straightened, the aged vampire breathed a deep sigh of despair, and a single tear formed in the corner of his eye There was no point in looking further, he concluded. The world had thoroughly, and utterly, destroyed itself, and every living soul had perished! Brushing the tear aside, Dracula knew that only one priority remained - survival, and that a hospital, or clinic, was likely to have what he needed . . . blood!

The Red Cross's make-shift hospital in Times Square provided an excellant source for his nourishment. Although the shelves and storeroom were cluttered with broken glass and debris, he found several undamaged bottles of O-type blood in a small refrigerator. The vampire never bothered to check if the blood was still fresh; he simply emptied a cardboard box of bandages and carefully began to fill it with the precious containers. Then, as he reached for the last bottle, he heard a strange noise from outside the small storeroom.

Count Dracula whirled, with animal-like reflexes, into a crouch and bared his sharp fangs, hissing almost instinctively.

Seconds later, an enormous, half-mad dog sprang from the shadows, and advanced rapidly with an angry snarl. The mongrel hound was nearly a skeleton, its ghost-gray fur covered with cancerous sores and radiation burns. Saliva dripped from its swollen tongue, and its glazed eyes had turned blood-red. Supremely confident of the kill, the dog growled in anticipation, then lunged for the vampire.

Dracula caught the animal in mid-flight with his powerful hands and wrestled the dog to the ground. The two adversaries struggled, tumbling across the storeroom in deadly combat. The vampire heard an unidentified crash, glanced up, and realized that his precious bottles of blood had overturned. Angered, he back-handed the animal across its snout and momentarily stunned it. The Count then lashed out and seized the dog's throat in a vise-like grip, crushing its wind-pipe. Its ferocious jaws snapped one final time, and the mongrel hound went limp in the vampire's grasp, dropping to the floor.

Slowly, Count Dracula staggered to his feet, leaning heavily on the wall. He felt very much like a weary old man, sick to death of the endless struggle. He felt very much like what he was. Lifting his hands in exasperation, the vampire looked down at the animal's body. The smell of fresh blood aroused him, and he knelt beside the dog, drinking greedily to satisfy his unique hunger.

The aged vampire then went back to his burial vault and sifted through the thin layer of Transylvanian soil in his coffin. He feared that his revered homeland was now nothing more than a radioactive wasteland, like New York City. He felt alone - a:stranger in a strange land, and as he reclined in his crypt, memories of the past plunged him into deepest sorrow. He had endured so many centuries of loneliness and had known so many women, yet he had loved only once. Tormented, he thought of her as he drifted off to sleep.

*   *   *   *   *

Her voice called to him from the darkness. Then, as an amorphous shadow thickened and solidified, she stood quietly over him. Her dark hair fell softly on her shoulders, and her face and hands were pale against the vivid redness of her lips. She wore a transparent, ghost-white chemise that flowed and billowed as a heavy fog enveloped the burial vault.

"Mina, is that you .. ?" Dracula asked, bleary-eyed and confused, as if in a drunken stupor.

"Yes, my darling," she replied, comforting him.

"But how did you survive the .."

She raised a finger to her lips and urged him to silence. Mina then smiled knowingly, unfastening her night-gown as she drew nearer. She advanced slowly, erotically, captivately him with her hungry, passionate eyes, and Dracula watched her in disbelief. Finally, after removing the chemise, she traced the out-line of her body--from her thighs to her breasts--with an inviting, sensual sweep of her fingertips. "I have been waiting for you for a long time."

Count Dracula reached up to touch her cheek, but her ghostly apparition suddenly changed from a beautiful, womanly face into a sneering death's head. He recoiled in horror, hissing involuntarily, and awoke to realize that it was only a nightmare.

Light-headed and very weak, the aged vampire clumsily stepped from the narrow coffin and rested against the vault's heavy iron doors. Apparently, the dog's tainted blood had caused him to hallucinate, and had diminished his strength. Like his ancestors before him, Dracula, too, had fallen victim to a contaminated food source; and if he was to survive, it was imperative that he find a fresh, purified blood supply.

*　*　*　*　*

Relentlessly, like an animal stalking its prey, Count Dracula scoured the city for the precious fluid. He looked in hospitals, blood banks, donor centers, and free clinics, but all he found was stale blood that had gone un-refrigerated. Everywhere he turned, the spectre of death lurked hungrily. He would have settled for plasma and a little distilled water; however, he refused to be reduced to eating insects, like his former servant Renfield. What if he could find no other sustenance? Dracula suppressed a cold shiver and took a deep breath; he didn't want to think about that. Dracula pushed the fear to the back of his mind, and descended into the darkness of the city.

The aged vampire spent three weeks - almost the limit of his endurance - digging unsuccessfully through the ruins of the once-great metropolis. Finally, in a state of near total collapse, he stumbled across a research laboratory in lower Manhattan that was still functioning. Emergency lights, strobing a dull red, greeted him as he staggered through the rubble. The lab, which had been equipped with a desiel generator for emergencies, continued to operate without the instructions, or interference, of human beings. Although broken test-tubes and decaying bodies littered the floor, silent, mechanical workers maintained schedules and persisted in their research to find a cure for leukemia. Apparently, the building had been shielded from the Bomb's thermal pulse, and no one had bothered to dismiss the loyal workers when doomsday arrived. He would have laughed at the irony of the moment, but his hunger superseded all other thoughts and emotions.

Moving unsteadily toward the lab's refrigerator, Dracula licked his lips in anticipation, and carefully examined each of the bottles inside. The blood was still fresh and had not been contaminated by experimentation. He breathed a sigh of relief, then gorged himself on several bottles, drinking the fluid, as though it were a magic elixir of life.

In one corner of the room, Count Dracula sat back contentedly, and felt something wondrous stir inside his body. As he closed his eyes to rest, the blood restored color to his pale, death-like features and rejuvenated his cadaverously thin body. The aged vampire had survived extinction one more time!

*   *   *   *   *

Count Dracula awoke to discover several empty faces looking down upon his own. He shivered slightly, sat up, then uttered a nervous sigh of surprise and anguish. It was only the silent laboratory workers. Even though the vampire had only a limited knowledge of computers and robotics, he made use of the available technical manuals and taught the silent workers to perform a series of rudimentary tasks. He bestowed names upon each of them - borrowed from recent memory - and assigned them chores, based on individual character traits: the robot, he named Dr. Van Helsing, was brooding and self-important, and was given the responsibility of reconstituting the lab's dried blood; Jonathan Harker, studious and business-like, maintained the generator and office equipment; Dr. Seward, fastidious and exacting, removed the decaying bodies and cleaned the lab. And Renfield, attentive yet slow-witted, was made his personal manservant and entrusted with the task of relocating the vampire's tattered belongings.

With the help of his silent servants, Dracula spent the afternoon building a new world. He realized that he was not an artist, yet, by preying upon man's culture (much like he had once preyed upon man) , he became a virtuoso, creating order out of chaos. He surrounded himself in a luxury that he had not known for several hundred years. He rescued Picassos, Matisses and Rembrandts from the rubble of the Metropolitan Museum of Art, preserved the music of Mozart, Beethoven and Wagner, and retrieved, from the smoldering fires at the great library, Goethe's *Faust*, Milton's *Paradise Lost*, T.S. Eliot's *The Wasteland*, and other literary classics. His home was transformed into a treasure trove, the last bastion of intellectual and aesthetic enlightenment in the new Dark Ages, and he was once again a monarch supreme.

But, as Dracula relaxed in his new surroundings and watched Renfield and the others complete their assigned tasks, he knew that he was still alone. The smell of lubrication and the discharge of static electricity reminded him that his silent servants were not alive and that, if he suddenly died, they would continue working, forever! He was jealous of their mechanized existence, and he looked upon their interaction and purpose with great envy. They did not need blood to maintain their immortality, like he did, and their lives were not dependent upon him. His servants were in name only, functioning as constant reminders of his loneliness.

Three days later, annoyed with their independence, the aged vampire terminated their "life" functions and destroyed their nuclear batteries.

*   *   *   *   *

During the night, another radiation storm--with high, swirling winds that blew particles of fall-out--struck New York and deposited a thin layer of radioactive dust across the cityscape. Count Dracula spent a restless, tossing night, listening to the tortuous sounds of the distant storm. He had never become accustomed to the hissing sounds of the whirlwind and the flashes of lightening without thunder or rain, and he struggled - with great difficulty - to sleep through the radiation storm. Half the night he lain awake, staring at the blank ceiling, trying to forget his loneliness; but he was unable to get Mina out of his thoughts, as the storm pounded his building. Then, for awhile, in between winks of sleep, he imagined holding her tightly in his arms; but as the storm raged on, reality wrenched her away.

Startled out of an uneasy sleep, Dracula irritably sat up   in his coffin and took deep breaths of the darkness. He then looked stiffly around the laboratory and realized that Mina was nowhere to be found; she had only appeared in a ghastly nightmare. If only he had completed her conversion process, she, too, would have been a vampire, and he would not have been alone.

"If only —" the aged vampire whispered between clenched teeth, as he stepped from his coffin and stood in the center of the room. He knew that the nightmares were coming more often and were getting much worse; and, as he glimpsed the lifeless bodies of his servants in one corner of the laboratory, he questioned his own sanity. He had taken their "lives" indiscriminately in a fit of rage, and the thought of random, purposeless violence was hateful to him.

Dracula wanted to cry, but the hollowness in his breast was dry and cold. How much more of this shallow existence did he have to endure?

Hanging his head in surrender, the aged vampire walked crest-fallen into the dead metropolis. Despair and anguish flooded his thoughts. He paused momentarily at the entrance of a parking garage, then covered his face against the darkness. Count Dracula felt that he had reached the end of   his life, and that he could no longer survive--alone. He also knew that the blood supply (in the laboratory) was not endless and that eventually he would have to search for more. He refused to go through that nightmare again, and finally, he concluded that death was infinitely preferable to life without meaning.

As Dracula turned to leave, he sensed movement from behind him in the garage. Then, suddenly, he felt two sharp pincers claw at his jacket and heard the fine cloth ripping away in their clutches. Dracula whirled around, and instinctively struck out at the unknown with his powerful fists. He imagined - in that   frozen instant - seeing his former nemesis Dr. Van Helsing, with crucifix in hand; but as the reality of the moment seized him , his heart sank, and he fell heavily back against the wall, hands trembling. He had just taken the "life" of another robot.

Anger overwhelmed him, then, moments later, as he looked

upon the mechanical being, thoughts of bewilderment filled him with new energy. He realized that this was no ordinary robot. It was a survey robot - the type used in hostile environments - and it was not programmed to function independently. Someone had to have dispatched the robot—perhaps other survivors.

The vampire breathed a sigh of renewed hope.

*   *   *   *   *

That afternoon, he watched the robot's body closely, with great anticipation, confident that its owners would attempt to   reclaim it~ Since he did not want to be seen, Dracula crouched beneath the fallen marquee signs of Broadway and settled back under the cover of darkness. He spent the afternoon and part   of the night thinking of the possibilities. He had missed the companionship of humans, even if they were weak and very destructive creatures, and he welcomed the though of fellow survivors.

Twelve hours passed, then fifteen. His mind became fatigued, thinking about the robot, as he tried to suppress the thought that no one was coming. Dracula forced those doubts away, grimly conscious that he dared not loose hope in this last desperate attempt for personal preservation; the other way - if he lost hope - offered only despair and an eternity of loneliness. Somehow, he knew that there were others alive, and he was determined to wait until one of them showed.

He did not have to wait long.

Far down the street, a black shadow moved, and a solitary figure emerged from the rubble of the metropolis. The aged vampire peered through the darkness, but he could not make out any details about the figure. It was too dark, and he could barely see his own hand in front of his face.

Breathing softly, Dracula moved slowly with animal stealth toward the figure, focusing all his attention and cunning on his objective. He silently wished that all the powers attributed to him by Bram Stoker. and other authors was true. He could not dissolve into a bat, or metamorph into a wolf, or walk through walls; but secretly he knew that he would not need any of those abilities. Pausing in the shadows, he studied the human, and fought back the natural urge to pounce upon him for fresh blood.

The man wore a yellow radiation suit, complete with helmet and oxygen tanks, and carried a sophisticated tracking device and Geiger counter. As he knelt over the remains of the survey robot, he regarded the mechanical man with pity and astonishment. He could not determine any signs of a struggle, or discover any reason for an attack. The man then adjusted the harness of his pack and glanced at the pressure gauge; time was running short, and he had only a few moments remaining to complete his examination before he had to return.

Dracula could tell that he was visibly distressed, as the man stood and looked up-and-down the street. He hesitated and wondered aloud what could have attacked his robot so savagely.

Sensing imminent danger, the man instantly came on guard and hurried across the boulevard, heading back in the direction that he had come.

The aged vampire followed closely behind, blending into the shadows, making certain that he was not seen but resolute   not to loose his prey.

Traversing the complex maze of rubble and destruction, the two survivors - one human and one vampire - traveled through the dead metropolis. For a while, their measured footsteps joined in unison as one echo, which pulsated like a heartbeat in the darkness. The man maintained a steady pace and moved swiftly, yet with great caution, towards his secret dwelling. But Dracula, panting, struggling for each new breath, could not keep up; he was not used to strenuous exercise anymore, like he once had been before the holocaust, and he quickly fell behind.

However, as the aged vampire slowed, he noticed that the man had left a clear trail of footprints in the radioactive dust. Catching his breath, he thanked the providence of the recent storm, then he continued his pursuit of the human survivor. Much further down the street, in front of the ruins of Penn Station, the man began to slow his pace. Only when he   had reached the entrance to the building - a vantage point that somehow gave him a feeling of security and power - did he pause and look back. Glancing left and right, the man checked to see if he had been followed. Then, satisfied that he wasn't, he took a deep breath, and carefully examined his pressure gauge. He was nearly out of oxygen and had reached the maximum exposure level to radiation.

Count Dracula advanced to within twenty-five feet of his objective and gingerly evaded his glance by crouching in the shadows. Then, after the man had climbed through the rubble and debris of the doorway, Dracula slipped into one of the lesser-used entrances. He surveyed the deserted train station, his animal-like senses questing, looking, listening for a noise that would betray the location of his prey. Moments later, he heard the man's footsteps, as they cast a variety of echoes in the death-like silence, and he followed the sounds through the ruins of the building and down a near-by esculator.

The aged vampire traveled down many levels, from street level to sub-basement, plunging into the very depths of the earth. As he descended lower and lower into the station, he began to recognize certain life-signs,. first, and foremost, he saw garbage, tons of refuse that had collected over the last few months; and then he came upon huge, lead-lined containers of food and sanity goods. He realized that there were enough supplies to support a small colony of fifty-to-sixty humans for a period of five or six years.

Finally, Count Dracula reached the lowest level. He searched in one direction after another, and eventually he found the man in the radiation suit. His heart gladdened at the sight, and he moved toward his objective with quick and eager expectation. But when he progressed closer, the man disappeared down a long ramp into a dark subterranean vault.

At the entrance to the ramp the aged vampire hesitated in thoughtful reflection. He was no longer alone! He had discovered - to his delight - that there were other survivors - of the atomic war, and he offered to build them a new world - a planet of vampires. By converting some of them, they would no longer be subject to the lethal effects of radiation and they could once again move about freely on the surface; the others would be kept and bred as cattle. He suspected that the nuclear winter would last for several years, and together they could create a brave, new world, free of the push-button wars and rampant technology that had nearly destroyed the world.

Count Dracula, the last surviving vampire, descended into the darkness, and the cycle began again.

The Second Apple

■

"The Second Apple" was one of my first professional stories, and when I look back on it from a perspective of twenty-five years, I just shake my head and wonder what the hell I was thinking about! The story, as I dimly recall, is actually a later draft of a much earlier work I had written in college; the first draft was well-received by my professor and classmates, and was published in the literary magazine. At the time I first wrote it, I had just finished reading A Canticle for Leibowitz, *and was quite taken by Walter M. Miller's religious symbolism. In the Hugo Award-winning novel, Catholic priests try to piece together 20th Century America six hundred years after an atomic war has bombed them back to the Middle Ages. "The Second Apple" was my first post-holocaust story, thanks in some part to the set-up in Miller's work.*

Trajan, barely listening to the crackle of remote voices in his space helmet, turned toward the horizon to greet the dawning sun, and breathed a deep sigh of awe. In the distance, the hyacinth blue mountains had erupted from the darkness to embrace the pale yellow sunlight, and a purple tide was flowing up from the valley, crashing like the waves of a great ocean of light against the dark, shadowy landscape. He marveled as the night created the day, giving form and substance to the wasteland. On the more gentle slopes, he imagined he could hear the echoes of those enticing sirens of Titan with their fatal love song of immortality. He then looked down, and before him, a series of footprints, stretching out in several directions from his space ship, had given the bare shapeless form of the moon some character, some substance.

He continued to survey the moonscape, and all at once, a light glistened from the darkness. Suddenly, his pastoral thoughts were a jumbled chaos of ideas. He squinted, looking at it long and hard, then realized its importance.

"Out there—almost to the horizon!" cried Trajan to his men.

Domitian and Faunus, his fellow cosmic travelers, turned in slow motion, as if performing an obscure ballet in the lower gravity of the lunar surface.

In the foreground, the reflection became more intense, the harsh glare of the sun blinding his field of vision. He studied the strange remoteness of the light. It was terribly simple, he reassured himself; macabre parodies of life always have an explanation. He shook his head, wetting his dry lips with an equally dry tongue. His mouth tasted like burnt rubber and his stomach was sick from the stale, recirculating air in his oxygen tank

Another glance. His men had turned, but their overt gestures communicated their confusion more than the raising crescendo of words on his intercom. Wait! Walt! He started to slow down his mind, slow down their confused cries, slow events down to a single moment. Can't they see it? he thought. Don't they realize what it means?

"There," he exclaimed, pointing towards the sunrise. "There it is! Sitting almost on the horizon." Looking again, Trajan saw a metallic object, cylindrically shaped, perhaps a ship or some other kind of structure. An alien craft? A forgotten lunar civilization? No, he said silently to himself. For some reason, which was buried deep within him, he knew that it was more than an alien craft or a forgotten city. He didn't know how he knew; he just simply knew that it was a reminder of a world which his people had buried a thousand years before.

Reflected in his eyes was a lost terror, the cornerstones of a dead world. He imagined seeing Thanatos leading a turbid cast of players in a somber funeral dirge: Prometheus carrying the fabled gift of fire, Tantelus and the secrets of Zeus, Moses talking to the burning bush, Bellerophon proudly saddled upon Pegasus, the winged-horse, Odysseus weeping over the loss of his mighty men, Christ nailed to a cross, Dante and Virgil carelessly trekking through Hell, Theseus displaying the head of Minos, Phaeton riding the chariot of Apollo, Beowulf fighting Grendel, Thor and his mighty hammer, Washington crossing the Delaware, Tarzan swinging through the trees with the apes, Tom, Huck, Jim, and the whole meandering Mississippi. . . . One by one, they came, streaming from the pages of a history long lost. Finally, he saw Harmony carrying the scales of justice in one hand and the horn of plenty in the other. The gleam in Trajan's eyes widened as the danse macabre marched by him and his men.

Once the spectacle had passed, Trajan turned toward his two fellow travelers. He wanted to reassure them, to say the things that Captains always say to their crews, but he couldn't seem to find the words. He immediately extinguished any thoughts about it for fear that he himself might become part of that curious parade. The sense of unreality made him feel as if he was acting a part that had nothing to do with life at all, like he was a player on some grand cosmic stage. Of course, it had to be a fantasy, a hallucination of some sort, he thought, shaking his head.

Domitian drew two or three deep breaths, then said, "Captain, what the hell was that?"

"I don't know," Trajan replied. "I've never seen anything like it before—" His voice trailed off, and became a series of crackles in static.

Faunus grabbed Trajan by his arm and said, "I think we better call Mission Control. They'll know what to do!"

"I hope you're right—"

*   *   *   *   *

"This is Mission Control at 119 hours, 22 minutes Ground Elapsed Time into the flight of *Pathos Seven*-the first manned mission to the Moon," said Territan, voice of Mission Control from Houston, Texas. "During these past several hours, we have had a very thorough communications check with the space craft. The crew appears to be in top physical condition and there been no serious problems. Right at this moment, the Flight Director has advised me that the men are performing certain routine mapping and surveying experiments on the lunar surface. . ."

Primus, the Flight Director and operational head of the Space Project, walked past the television cameras and the news commentators, looking cynically at them. What the hell did they know, he thought, examining his chronometer. No, dammit, the year was still 1174, even though it seemed to him light years later. His eyes sparkled at the thought, and then faded to anxiety once more. He continued across the long room, and then stopped to speak with Territan as he concluded his briefing.

"Okay," snapped Primus, "let me have it. What's the problem?"

"Well, boss, I know you're not going to like this," he said, avoiding eye contact with his superior. "But, our boys have found something."

"Found something," Primus repeated. "Found what?"

Territan's head bent down, and he stared in long abstraction at his toes. He was afraid to answer for fear that his boss might not like it.

"Answer me!" he demanded. "What did they find?"

"That's just it! We haven't got the damnedest idea what it is," he replied with a trace of embarrassment. "We were hoping that you would talk to them."

Primus took a few forward steps, then stopped. "Switch on channel number 4. I'll speak to them from this console." He clenched his teeth, and as he breathed, the air hissed in and out like some kind of serpent. "Trajan, what the hell is going on? Is this some kind of practical joke, or what?"

The Mission Control room was dead silent.

"Negative, CapCom. There is something out there!"

The Flight Director started to say something, but was abruptly cut off by a crackling voice from the radio monitor.

"Don't ask me what the hell it is, CapCom," Trajan continued. "I wouldn't know where to begin to explain."

"What did you find? Can you describe it to me!" Primus persisted. "What does it look like?"

"The structure itself is cylindrical in shape," Trajan replied, his words shallow and empty of meaning, as if he was drugged. "But I'll be damned if I can tell what the hell came out of it just a few moments ago."

Hammering the "off" button with his fist, the Flight Director disconnected his audio connection with the lunar crew. "Goddammit—he doesn't make any sense!" he exclaimed. "Why can't he tell me what's going on. Surely, it must look like something!" To one of the technicians, he ordered, "I want you to pull the plates and stills of that region immediately."

"Yes, sir."

"We'll get a good look at whatever it is," he said, grinning.

Territan approached the center console. "I don't remember seeing any cylindrical objects in the photos. Suppose, they don't show us anything?"

"What are you babbling about now?"

"I just asked you what would happen if the plates showed up negative," he replied, somewhat hesitantly.

"Nothing," he said rather abruptly, "because they won't."

Moments later, the technician returned with several plates and stills, and started to place them on the center console. Primus looked down his nose at him, plucking the photos out of his hand. Black and white stills and negative plates, emphasizing the lunar landscape, but void of any object or abstraction.

Primus's eyebrows stitched together. "But that's im—"

"Impossible?" Territan mused.

The Flight Director looked more closely, and suddenly an image thickened and solidified on one of the photographs. "Impossible," he said, biting his lower lip. "A moment ago, that wasn't there—"

Territan looked over his shoulder. "Omigod."

"We can't be certain, but it does look like the great prophesy has come true. Contact Trajan immediately, and have him return to his ship with his crew. We've got to get them out of there as soon as possible!" Primus turned to his technician. "When's the next available launch window?"

"Seventy-two hours," the technician replied.

"That's not soon enough," he exclaimed. The Flight Director turned away from the center console, and looked at the red telephone. "I've got to call the Chairman of the Unified Status immediately. We've got to get our people to high sanctuary. There's just so little time left to prepare."

*   *   *   *   *

Trajan and his crew disobeyed the orders from Mission Control, and once they had replenished their oxygen supply, went back out to explore the strange, cylindrical object.

The sun was higher now in the lunar sky as the three cosmic travelers made their way across the barren wasteland. For an instant, Trajan marveled at the thought of being in perpetual daylight for several weeks. It was a haunting feeling which awed and amused him at the same time. But he had little time for amusement. Before him lay the strange, cylindrical object. . . partially buried in the lunar surface by rock and debris, it could have been an alien spacecraft or some building or structure from a lost civilization. He stroked its surface, rubbing the cosmic dust away from its metallic frame, and in doing so, uncovered a collection of hieroglyphs and pictographs. The symbols meant nothing to him, but as he rubbed further, he discovered a series of alphanumeric characters. The letters and numbers did seem familiar; they were an ancient language known as English.

"United States," he struggled with the words on the legend. *"United States Moon Lab. Established in 2028 by the National Aeronautical and Space Administration (N.A.S.A.) for the benefit of all peoples of the Earth."*

Domitian and Faunus had stopped cold in their tracks, as Trajan retreated from the structure.

"2028. Oh, my God!" he exclaimed.

"Lunar base," Primus's voice crackled in their headphones. "This is Houston, CapCom. Do you read me? Over."

Silence—dead silence.

"Dammit, Trajan! Respond!"

"Roger, CapCom," he replied, forcing the lump back down in his throat.

"Are you prepared for lift-off?"

"Negative, CapCom," Trajan said, as he glanced from Domitian to Faunus. He knew he was going to have to tell Primus the truth, whether he liked it or not. "My crew and I have gone EVA to have closer look at the object "

"What! Didn't I give you a direct order to return to the ship?"

"That's affirmative, CapCom," he responded, his voice cracking. "But we just couldn't follow that order, and abandon one of the great discoveries."

After another moment of silence, Primus asked, "Well, what

did you find?"

"It appears to be some type of buried structure," he lied, then thought better of his lie. "No, check that. It's really a lunar base of some kind, packed with life support systems. Human life support systems. The legend reads, '*United States Moon Lab. Established in 2028 by the National Aeronautical and Space Administration (N.A.S.A.) for the benefit of all peoples---*'"

Primus replied, under his breath, "Oh, my God."

"The evolutionists were right!" His lips were stiff as he spoke. "We did descend from a lower form of animal life—man!"

Trajan turned, hardly listening to the garbled words which were coming from his helmet, but aware, simply, that he was right. He walked slowly around the building, cautious and curious at the same time. He reached for the door-handle of an airlock, and pulled on it. The airlock came open with a hiss. Trajan reached for a flashlight, and shined its narrow beam in front of him as he inspected the chamber. Just then, he froze in terror.

"It can't be. It just can't be!"

Domitian hurried to his side, leaving Faunus behind to stand guard on the lunar sand. "What in God's name is that?"

"God doesn't have anything to do with it."

"What is it?" Primus scowled.

Trajan whirled. "Get the hell out of my head, Primus. Will you!"

"Domitian," he demanded, "What is it?"

"It is a tri-colored flag—red, white and blue." His voice shook with terror and disbelief. "It has thirteen stripes—seven red and six white. I'd swear that it was an exact replica of the one which was told of in our folklore the one carried by the whore of Babylon." He suddenly faded back to the years of his childhood, remembering the ghastly stories which his parents told him in the night. "I can still recall the story of the coming of the heavenly bomb, delivered from the firmament of the heavens."

Back in Mission Control, the Flight Director grimaced for he remembered the same story: the coming of the bomb, the burning and destruction of the old world, the casting out of evil, and the creation of the new Adam and the new Eden. His mouth hung open in awesome puzzlement, realizing for the first time in his life that the story of creation was more than a simple fairytale. Primus sobered up.

"You've got to get back to the ship, Domitian," he commanded, the words crackling as they traveled across the thousands of miles of space. "You have no idea what kind of danger you're in, so I'm ordering you back to the ship."

Domitian received his orders, but chose not to follow them. Instead, he and Trajan penetrated the outer chamber of the moon lab, and made their way into the central core of the station. They couldn't help but feel scared. After all, their whole discovery had been prophesied over a thousand years before. They continue to investigate the structure. All of the instruments were covered with a thick dust, and the badly decomposed remains of a human were stretched across a central control panel.

"Poor devil," Domitian remarked

"It's a damned humanoid," Trajan said flatly. "What a hideous creature it must have been!"

"What should we do with it?"

"Let it rot! Who gives a damn!"

Trajan then fingered a button on the console, and the instruments came alive, buzzing and whirring like some primitive lifeform of its own. He glanced up at Domitian, then scowled with laughter. "Damn thing still works," he declared.

"Must be powered by some kind of solar or nuclear battery," his crewman stated, pushing buttons of his own. "I just can't believe the equipment still works after all this time. Is that really possible?"

Trajan shrugged his shoulders. He continued pushing buttons, while he ignored the voices he heard from Earth. Then he heard a new voice, distant and muffled through his space helmet, but a new voice all the same. He quickly attached a series of relays which would connect him to the primitive equipment. Smiling grimly at Domitian, he switched it on. . .

"Daily Log. July 11, 2031, Commander Steve Arthur reporting. I will continue recording until the equipment fails or I am dead. Not quite the most optimistic thing to say, but frankly I don't give a damn any more. Nothing matters! Item: in less than thirty-six hours my oxygen will be exhausted, including the reserve in my own tanks. Item: the food and water will also be gone. And then I will begin to rot, forcing my mind to vegetate upon my worthless body. Not exactly a fun way to die--"

"Take him off S band and put him on VHF," shouted the Flight Director to one of the technicians back at Mission Control. He pulled at his collar. His shirt was drowning in a pool of dehydrated fluids. "Copy this. I want every word that is said recorded from this point on!"

"—war, utter futility," Commander Arthur continued, "the dreaded conflict of nuclear and chemical/biologic war has finally come. No, not just a simple border skirmish, but total commitment! The Iranian-Iraqi Alliance launched a full-scale attack on Israel, following the breakdown of the Lewinsky Accords, and the United States had little choice but to support their lifelong allies. The war lasted less than two hours, and now, three days later as I look down upon the Earth, a great radioactive shroud covers the entire planet. Nuclear winter, no. Just nuclear death and destruction."

Domitian looked to Trajan for help in understanding some of the unfamiliar words, but the Captain merely stood silent, lost in his thoughts.

"I look out into space, watching the shadow of the moon as it slowly devours the Earth, For the first time in my life, I feel lonely," the recording continued. "I tried calling London last night, but no one answered. I tried calling Sydney this morning, but there wasn't even a crackle. I can envision the deserted cities, paper flying freely down the equally deserted streets, occasionally stopping to look at an abandoned car. The grocery store around the corner is overrun with rats and other vermin. The unburied dead are cloistering at the local church or synagogue— each waiting their turn for absolution. And the factories—all void of life, of purpose, of volition, even of hostility. Simply one huge, dead, immeasurable steam engine rolling on, in its dead indifference. . ."

Trajan stopped the recording.

"This is Houston, CapCom," Primus said dully. "What happened to the recording?"

"The recording seems to have stopped," Trajan lied. He hurried Domitian out of the room, and added, "My men and I are awaiting instructions."

"I've been ordered to attend a special meeting of the war department. It appears that your·discovery has triggered a major international incident in the Middle East," the Flight Director explained. "I'll get back to you with lift-off instructions in a few hours. In the meantime, you should cover the body and seal off the building. The mystery is over."

"Is it, Primus?" Trajan said under his breath, but before his superior could respond, both Domitian and Faunus cut into their conversation.

"Captain--"

"Captain, you're not going to believe this."

"What is it, now?" the Captain returned, annoyed.

"We've found another body."

*   *   *   *   *

Several hundred feet from the moon lab, Domitian and Faunus had discovered the remains of another human. Fragments of its skeletal structure were partially buried under some rock and cosmic dust, but it was definitely human. The Captain examined the remains, from head to foot, and shook his head in disbelief.

"We found it on the far side of the moon lab," Trajan reported. "It's definitely the remains of another human, but how it got here is beyond me. There's no evidence of a spacesuit or any other kind of environmental apparatus. How the poor devil got out here is a mystery in itself. By all rights, he couldn't have survived more than a few feet."

"Cover it up, and return to your ship," the Flight Director ordered, his voice suddenly fading.

"That's just it, Houston, we don't dare cover it up," Trajan replied in an unsteady tone. He struggled to regain composure, but was overwhelmed by this tidal wave of emotion. Finally, he said, "There are something like shackles on its feet, and those shackles seem to be bolted to a rock on the lunar surface--"

"That's enough, Trajan."

"--and there's something in its hand."

"I said that's enough," Primus shouted, his voice crackling through their headphones. "I want all of you to get back to the ship right now!"

"It's an apple, CapCom—a damned apple!" Trajan said, in total disbelief. "It's suspended in a transparent cube of glass, and an inscription, in English, on the side reads, 'And in those days shall men seek death, and shall not find; and shall desire to die, and death shall flee from them.'"

Back in Mission Control, Primus slumped down in his chair, now oblivious to his surroundings, the burden of the entire planet upon his shoulders. His eyes wallowed in an arbitrary land where the sky was blue and the cities old. He knew the bombs would be falling soon, and all that would be left of him or that place would be distant memories. He smiled faintly, but said nothing for he had finally recalled the words of the last prophesy: "And they marched up over the broad earth and surrounded the camp of the saints and the beloved city; but fire came down from Heaven and consumed them, and the devil who had deceived them was thrown into the lake of fire and brimstone where the beast and the false prophet were, and they will be tormented day and night for ever and ever. . ."

About the Author

John L. Flynn, Ph. D. was born in Chicago, Illinois, in 1954. He earned a BA and MA in English at the University of South Florida. He received the M. Carolyn Parker Award for outstanding journalism for his freelance work on several Florida daily newspapers. He sold his first book, *Future Threads*, in 1985, and became a member of the Science Fiction Writers of America in 1986. In 1987, John served as the educational consultant on *The Dictionary of Essential English*. He has subsequently published a number other books, including *Cinematic Vampires* (1992), *Phantoms of the Opera: Behind the Mask* (1993), *The Films of Arnold Schwarzenegger* (1993), *Dissecting Aliens* (1995), *War of the Worlds: From Wells to Spielberg* (2005), *The Jovian Dilemma* (2006), *75 Years of Universal Monsters* (2006), *50 Years of Hammer Horror* (2007), *101 Superheroes of the Silver Screen* (2007), *2001: Beyond the Infinite* (2008), *Intimate Bondage* (2014) and its four sequels in the Kate Dawson series. In 1997, he earned a doctorate in clinical psychology from Southern California University, and published the *Etiology of Sexual Addiction: Childhood Trauma as a Primary Determinant.* With Bob Blackwood, he wrote *Everything I Know About Life I Learned from James Bond* and *Future Prime: The Top Ten Science Fiction Films* (both in 2015). Today, retired from the University of Maryland system after thirty-five years of loyal service, John continues to write full time, and makes his home in Lake Worth, Florida.